The Real Housewives

of

Adverse City 2

SCANLIFE

Get more Info About Shelia E. Bell books!

What Others Say About Books by Shelia E. Bell

"Shelia E. Lipsey is one of the few authors who sets my heart to blaze with her writing. Her writing is intense, complex, unforgettable and most of all, needed in the world today. Shelia's novels have everything Christian fiction novels need: brilliant plots, timely conversations, and faith building passages! Keep your eyes on Shelia E. Lipsey...she is definitely a legend in the making." --- Ella Curry, president of EDC Creations. Publisher of Black Pearls Magazine. Based on novels Beautiful Ugly and My Son's Wife

By Sherri Gregory March 27, 2016 "The Real Housewives of Adverse City) Shelia, you have done it again, your writing style, storyline and great details as always is above and beyond . From page one to the end, I was talking to myself and turning the page to see what are they going to do next? I got into each character individually and as couples, the drama and life situations are here and there is a lot! Everybody has a separate journey, and I can't wait to see how they handle this. Shelia, please come on with the next book. I can't give anything away (as bad as I want to, especially Pastor Carlton Porter- he is all over the place and he is spreading more than the gospel around). but I can tell you this please get your copy, I'm telling everybody I know this is a must read, you will enjoy.

The Life of Payne by Shelia E. Bell This book was clearly a tall tale of struggle, Payne and how much can one endure the hardships from as close as a family member as your mother. No matter what the main character did to earn her love, he still was pushed away. Sadly, this fictional story is all too real for many individuals that have family members that are addicted to drugs or just blatantly lost their way. Shelia Bell knows how to flesh out the most from her characters so that she can deliver the best to her readers. Superb job, looking forward to reading more from this author. Amazon Reviewed by Michael D. Beckford, Author of "Little Black Bird"

The Real Housewives

of
Adverse City 2

Shelia E. Bell

ISBN 978-1-944643-03-4

Library of Congress Control Number: 2017909288

Cover designed by The Final Wrap - Thefinalwrap.com

"Never let a problem to be solved become more important than a person to be loved." Barbara Johnson

DEAR GOD
I WANNA TAKE A MINUTE
NOT TO ASK FOR ANYTHING
BUT SIMPLY TO SAY
THANK YOU
FOR ALL I HAVE!
PLEASE LET ME NEVER FORGET
TO BE GRATEFUL
FOR THE THINGS I HAVE
AND PATIENT FOR THE THINGS I DON'T.

Chapter 1

"Sometimes the hardest part isn't letting go but rather learning to start over." Nicole Sobon

Meesha and her oldest sister, Geena, talked while she finished packing for her and the boys return trip to Adverse City. She'd been at Geena's house for the past two weeks which proved to be quite therapeutic.

Initially, she thought about not telling her sister anything about what had transpired, but with social media these days that was impossible. News about Carlton, Peyton, and now a dead Breyonna was still trending.

"I hope you at least think about some of what I said. Sometimes things aren't always as they seem, Meesha. Don't get me wrong. From what you told me, I see why you needed to get away, but by the same token, I think you should look at it from Carlton's view too."

"I don't see why I should look at it from Carlton's view. Nothing that man has said or done lately makes sense. I thought we had something special, Geena. I thought he really loved me. To find out that he's had a baby with Peyton; it's just too much."

"Girl, that was fifteen years ago. I'm not excusing what he did, but you all were freshly married, new in your relationship, and people mess up. I'm sorry to have to tell you that no one is perfect. But something inside of me tells me that Carlton is not all bad. I just think he made some bad choices."

Meesha stopped packing and sat down on the edge of the bed, holding one of her son's shirts in her hand. As she toyed with the shirt, she looked at her sister. "I want to believe that he's one of the good guys, I really do, but his actions say otherwise."

"Like I said, that boy you're talking about is half grown. And I think you should listen to Peyton. If she says they didn't sleep together, then accept that. Dang, why is it so hard to believe that she adopted the kid?"

"That's just it, Geena. It's hard to know what to believe. Seems like everyone has a lie on their lips these days. I don't know what to do and I don't know who to believe."

"It's horrible that that woman, Breyonna, who claimed she was Liam's mother, is dead. But the thing is, she never said anything about Peyton and Carlton sleeping together. She supposedly claimed the boy as her biological son. So why are you so upset? And why would Carlton just accept that woman's word that the boy is his son anyway? I don't care what kind of birthmark he has or how much he looks like Carlton; I would demand he take a DNA test. Are you crazy or what? Have you not seen Maury?"

Meesha jumped up off the bed and slung the shirt aside. "At the end of the day, Carlton betrayed me and so did Peyton. We're talking about my husband and one of my closest friends, Geena. Ugh, I can't believe you're on their side."

"I never said I was on anybody's side. All I want you to see is that things aren't just one sided here. You're angry, you're hurt, and you're pregnant, so everything is out of whack right now. You're not thinking rationally. What you need to be doing is praying about this whole situation. You're a woman of God. Where is your faith? I mean, look at all the times I've had to lean on you for some down to earth, Godly advice. I can rely on you to tell me the truth, even if it hurts. Well, I'm here to do the same for you. I just want you to open your eyes, think about this thing for a minute. That's all."

Meesha sat back down on the bed calmly. "I know, and I'm sorry. It's just that I wanted a forever kind of relationship and marriage. Now I'm pregnant with my fifth child by a man who wants out. It's just too much to handle right now. And how can I accept that boy if it turns out that he really is Carlton's son. Then again, I guess I wouldn't have to accept him since Carlton wants a divorce," Meesha said sadly.

"You're not going to get me to believe that Carlton really wants a divorce. I don't care what he says or how many times he's said it. It's probably because of all this drama. He was scared that you were going to leave him. You know how some men are, they run scared at the first sign of trouble. Anyway, you can do this. Just rely on God and your faith. Go back to Adverse City and face your problems. Everything is going to turn out the way that it should. You'll see," Geena said with conviction in her voice, hoping she was giving her sister sound advice.

Geena finished helping Meesha pack and then proceeded to take her and the boys to the airport.

"It was good seeing you and spending time with you and my nephews," Geena told her sister before exiting the car.

"The same here. I wish it had been more for pleasure than me needing an escape though."

"I'm just glad you know that I have your back. That's what family should be about. You know to call me if you need me."

"Yeah, I know, thanks." Meesha opened the door and got out of the car. "Boys, give your Aunt Geena a hug then help me get this luggage out of the trunk."

The four boys did as they were told. Meesha waved her last goodbye to her sister, sucked in her breath, and walked toward their gate.

"Time to face the piper," she said underneath her breath. "Come on, boys."

Chapter 2

"The wheel of change moves on, and those who were down go up and those who were up go down." Jawaharlal Nehru

While Meesha and the boys were on their way back to Adverse City, Carlton made a call to Peyton to check on how things were going between Derek and their son, Liam. Peyton hated that Derek left her when he discovered everything she told him about adopting Liam was a lie. Liam was hurt by the lies too, and was glad to go with the man he recognized as his father. Both father and son had enough of Peyton's drinking binges and her out of control behavior. But her bed of deceit and lies was the straw that broke the camel's back."

"Have you talked to either one of them at all?" Carlton asked Peyton on the phone.

"I talked to Liam for a few minutes yesterday. He was still distant and short with me. I think Derek is poisoning his mind."

"I doubt that. Liam is a teenager, Peyton. It's hard to tell what they think and feel. But to be honest, he is a bright young man. I don't think Derek is saying anything to make him feel any type of way toward you. Derek is a good guy. No matter what's happening between the two of you, and even if it does involve Liam, Derek is not going to bad mouth you to his son. You're the boy's mother, and I don't care if that's biological or not."

"Thanks, Carlton. I know you're going through your own drama, so for you to take time to check on me means a lot."

"I'm not just your friend, Peyton; I'm your spiritual leader, your pastor. It's what I'm supposed to do."

"Any word from Meesha?"

"Nope, but CJ texted me this morning and told me they would be home later today."

Eleven year old, CJ was the oldest of the Porter boys. Most of the time rather than call him by his name, which was Carlton, Jr. everyone called him CJ. The other three boys were eight-year-old Marlon, seven-year old Malik, and five-year old Micah.

"Umm, so he did, huh. Bet he's eager to get home so he can be with his friends," Peyton said.

"Maybe, but I bet Meesha told him to do it so she wouldn't have to talk to me directly. You know it really wasn't about her going to see Geena. I think her intent was to leave me. That's all to it. And I can't say I blame her."

"I wouldn't say she left you, Carlton or else she and the boys wouldn't be coming home. I think she just needed some time to gather her thoughts. I mean, so much has been going on in all of our lives lately and sometimes it gets a bit much. And you seem to forget that you did tell her more times than not that you wanted a divorce. Come on now," Peyton reminded. "Let's be for real."

"I had my reasons," Carlton said somberly.

"Whatever your reasons then that's on you, but I wish that she would hear me out though about you and me. I can't get her to listen long enough for me explain everything that went down with Liam."

"She doesn't want to hear any of it right now. I'm like you, but what can I say? You're right, I've been barking down her throat for the past couple of months about wanting a divorce. Then Breyonna shows up and throws the past up in both of our faces, and suddenly all our lives are screwed up."

"I know it's harsh of me to say, but Breyonna got what she deserved. I don't want to say that anyone deserves to be killed, but I'm telling you, Carlton, it's hard for me to feel bad about her being dead. She set out to destroy not just you and me, but she hurt her own son in the process. Why couldn't she see that some things are better left unsaid."

Peyton walked around the circumference of her bedroom, holding her iPhone to her ear while talking to Carlton. She wanted a shot of vodka so badly, but fought against the urge. She had promised herself that she would lay off the liquor for a while. Not that she believed she had a problem, but because

Derek didn't like her drinking and neither did Liam. It had only been a couple of days since her last drink, but she missed it. Drinking was her mode of relaxation. Some folks liked to smoke cigarettes, some liked to smoke weed, and some liked to eat or whatever. Her vice was enjoying a shot or two or three of vodka, kick back, read a book, and chill. What was so wrong with that?

"I don't want to say that she got what she deserved. But what I will say is that I'm glad this is over and we can start to try to rebuild from this point forward. I think you should sit down and tell Liam the truth, and Derek too, of course. Reassure him that you love him and that you did what you thought was best at the time. That's all you can do, Peyton. Just be transparent. You know what I mean?"

"Yeah, I know what you mean, to a certain extent, but we still have some explaining to do. Liam needs to know what your intentions are now as his biological father. All he knows is what the media has spilled, and you know how they over inflate everything they report. I think we need to sit down with him and listen to his feelings about all of this. It would be good if you took some of your own advice, too."

"Now I'm lost," Carlton said. "What are you talking about take some of my own advice?"

"I'm talking about you and this divorce crap. Breyonna is dead. Everybody knows now thanks to social media about the situation with Liam, you, and me, so you don't have a reason anymore to divorce Meesha. The two of you are meant for each other. She's the mother of your children, the first lady of Perfecting Your Faith, your rock. You two have been through some times far worse than this, Carlton. But for you to say that you wanted a divorce is wild. When Meesha first told me I was flabbergasted. I thought you had to be losing it or something." Peyton released a light hearted chuckle into the phone.

Carlton sat behind the desk at Perfecting Your Faith while he sipped on a cup of coffee and chatted with Peyton. If only she knew that it wasn't all because of the secrets about Liam, it was way bigger and it was also because he was feeling someone else. That someone else was Avery Mitchelson. But, strangely the more the dust began to settle about the Liam situation, and now that the boy's birth mother, Breyonna, was dead, things were beginning to feel different for Carlton. Being inside a 5,000 square foot house all alone, without his wife and his sons, gave him reason to pause and think about what he really wanted. He definitely wanted to be a man pleasing to God. Within, he knew he hadn't been acting as such. The mere fact that he had been less than the man he felt God desired and chose him to be was evident. He possibly had a son who was born out of his lust for other women and drugs during the time. Breyonna was the snake that came back to bite him for his adulterous, cheating ways. Now he was involved with his wife's good friend, Avery. He cared deeply for her. His life felt like one big routine and Avery added a spark to it. But God wasn't in agreement with his actions, that much Carlton knew.

"I have a lot to think about and so do you."

"Yeah, we do. I want my husband and son back. I want my life back, Carlton."

"I know, but like you told me, things will work themselves out. Some way, somehow. Anyway, I have a lot to get done today. I'll talk to you later."

"Yeah, me too. Talk to you later, and think about what I said."

They ended their call and Carlton laid his phone down on his desk, clasped his hands together and prayed. "I need you, Father God. I've messed up so much. My family is gone. My wife is unhappy and I'm unhappy. I don't know what to do. There's a teenage kid that may be my son. A woman is dead indirectly because of stupid decisions I've made. I ask you for wisdom."

A knock on his door interrupted his prayerful petition. "Come in," he said.

"Hey, what's up, bro?" It was Kingston, one of Carlton's three brothers.

Carlton had three brothers and one sister. Two of his brothers, Kingston and Martin, lived nearby in Miami and worked in the ministry at Perfecting Your Faith. His youngest brother and his sister lived in Nashville where his sister was a pastor and his brother worked in the ministry with her. He and his siblings had grown up in the church and were involved in the ministry in some shape or fashion. His father was a retired preacher and his mother a retired Sunday School teacher and public school educator. It had hurt them to hear the trouble their son had gotten himself in. Carlton hated that he had embarrassed his family and caused such havoc.

"What's up, Kingston?"

"I just came to stick my head in and check up on you. Any word from Meesha and the boys?" Kingston asked and stepped further into Carlton's office.

"Not a word from her, but CJ texted me and said they would be home later today."

"Have you tried calling her?"

"To be honest, no, I haven't."

Kingston took the liberty and sat down in the chair in front of Carlton's desk, crossed his legs, glanced at his cell phone and then focused back on Carlton.

"I don't understand you, man. What is up with you? I don't know the depth of what's going on with you and Meesha. It's not my business but I know that you wanting out of your marriage and with everything revolving around Peyton and her kid, it can't help but have an effect on your marriage and family life. That's just a given fact. "

Carlton toyed with the ink pen he had in his hand and nodded in agreement. "Yeah, definitely. Actually, I'm glad you stopped by. There's something I want to talk to you and Martin about, but I guess I'll have to settle for just you since Martin is out of town this week." Carlton laughed and Kingston smiled.

"Yeah, you got jokes, huh? I talked to him earlier. He said he's having a good time at the conference, learning a lot, doing a lot of networking."

"I'm glad to hear that. I'll call him later. I think it was a good decision to send him. He can learn a lot about how we can spread our evangelism ministry and outreach."

"I agree. So, cut through the chase. What do you want to talk about?"

"I'm ashamed to say this but I need to confide in someone I can trust."

"Well, that's me fa sho. What's going on, man?"

"I've been unfaithful."

"You've been what?"

"You heard me. I've been cheating on my wife and it's with one of her best friends."

"Man you've got to be kidding me. What is wrong with you? Who is it? Or do I even want to know? Is it Peyton, the one that's in the middle of all of this mess you're going through now?"

Carlton shook his head. "No, it's not her. We're not like that. She keeps trying to tell Meesha that, but Meesha won't listen."

"Do you blame her? I have a lot of respect for Meesha, man. Girl has been down with you from the get go. She's always had your back and she's involved in the ministry just as much as you are. I hate what's happening to the two of you. You and Meesha are me and Damica's example of how a marriage should be. You two have always been the ideal couple. When we get married in a few months, I can only hope that Damica will be in my corner the way Meesha is in yours. So why would you even do this?"

Carlton shook his head and extended his hands out in wonderment. "I don't know. It just happened. That's all I can tell you. But now I'm having second thoughts. I can't expect God's blessings if I'm involved in all of this mess, and adultery? My God what is wrong with me?"

"You're human. You gotta get past this. Anyway, who is she?"

"You can't tell a soul, not even Damica. Do you hear me? I like your girl. She's cool, but I'm sure even *you* will have to admit that she can't hold water so I know if she hears that I'm messing off, straight to her friends she'll go. And that means Meesha will know just as quickly."

"Yea, yea, yea. Now who is this woman that has you about to ruin your life and everything you've worked so hard to build?"

"Avery."

"Avery who? The only Avery I know is Avery Mitchelson."

Carlton looked at his brother with a guilty, dumbfounded expression.

"Man, don't tell me that. That woman is crazy as they come. Didn't she try to kill herself a few months ago? She's whacko."

"She is not whacko. And yes, she did try to commit suicide, but she was going through a lot. Her husband committed adultery on her and well a lot of things were out of place in her life. We had some counseling sessions about her depression and her problems, and—"

Kingston raised a hand. "Stop it, bro. I've heard it too many times....one thing led to another. Come on, man. Where is your self-control? And you just said for yourself that her husband cheated on her. So now you're going to help her do payback on him? Come on, Carlton. See that's why I've been so hesitant about jumping that broom. I don't want to cheat on Damica. She's a good girl. I wouldn't want to break her heart like that. It's why I had to be sure this is what I wanted before I asked her to marry me. You feel me?"

"Yea, but you just don't get it. Man, things happened so quick. But now that Meesha is gone, I realize how much I miss my wife, my kids, and my marriage. I miss life the way it used to be and I think I want that back."

"You think?" Kingston stood up, put one hand in his pocket and walked across the office floor. "You need to know, not think. You know God is not in this. So come on. Think about what you stand to lose here. And that kid, you need to get that straightened out too. You don't know for sure if he's even yours. A girl like Breyonna who was out in the streets doing drugs, there's no telling who she was laying with man. Anybody could be that boy's daddy."

"I know, I know. But I believe he's my kid."

"Whatever. I'm telling you, you need to be sure. And you need to think twice about destroying your family for some other female."

"I've been thinking about a lot of things since Meesha and the boys have been gone. I've repented to God and now I need to see if Meesha still wants me."

"So are you saying that you've ended it with Avery?"

Carlton hesitated before answering. "I'm going to do it today."

Kingston shook his head in disgust. "You need to do it today. Don't screw up your marriage and family over a piece of tail, especially a piece of crazy tail! Come on, now."

"I got it. I got it," answered Carlton, relieved that he'd confided in his brother.

Kingston walked to the door, opened it, stopped, and looked over his shoulder at his brother. "And another thing."

"What's that?"

"You need to do a legit DNA test. Not some 'I believe he's mine crap.' No telling who ole girl was messing around with out there in them streets. Be smart, bruh."

"Yeah, I hear ya. Thanks again, man."

"I'll holla at ya," Kingston said and walked out of Carlton's office.

Carlton contemplated everything his brother said. He knew it was time for him to talk to Avery. He had to put an end to things between them before they got to the point of no return. He'd already done too much by giving her that diamond Tiffany bracelet. He had confessed his love for her and now he had to break her heart by telling her that they needed to concentrate on their individual marriages and family. It was the right thing to do even though part of him wanted Avery. Was it lust or love? He wasn't sure but it was time to sacrifice his feelings for what he had been blessed with and that was the love of his wife and kids.

He also needed to talk to Peyton about getting a DNA test done on Liam. It was time he found out for sure if the kid was his. Just because the boy had a birthmark identical to his, or almost identical, didn't mean that he was his son. And if he was, it wasn't fair for Liam not to know for sure that he was his daddy.

Carlton picked up the phone to call Avery. Once he ended things with her, he could concentrate on getting his life back on track and hopefully establishing a relationship with Liam if the boy turned out to be his.

Chapter 3

"Anyone can possess, anyone can profess, but it is an altogether different thing to confess." Shannon L. Alder

Eva called Avery and Peyton to see if they wanted to meet up for lunch. It had been some time since they'd carried out the monthly routine of Ladies Day Out. She was tired of staying cooped up in a hotel and wanted the girls' advice about moving into her own house or townhome.

She couldn't expect to live in a fancy hotel forever, let alone raise a kid in a hotel. She still hoped that Harper would come around and they could work things out. Every day she expected a call from him telling her that he had made the whole thing up about having a vasectomy.

"I'm free," Avery told Eva when she called. "Where do you want to meet?"

"Do you even have to ask?" Eva replied.

"Zodiac Café?"

"You know it."

"Okay, have you talked to Peyton?"

"I sent her a text right before I called you. She said she could come. I just have to text her back and tell her that we're going to Zodiac."

"Do you want me to come by the hotel and pick you up?"

"No, I'm already out so I'll see you guys in say an hour. Is that cool?"

"Yeah, an hour is good for me."

"Okay, I'll text Peyton and let her know that we're meeting up at Zodiac in an hour. Bye."

"Bye," replied Avery.

Eva looked at her watch. She would have lunch with Avery and Peyton and later that afternoon she had her first doctor's appointment. She was both excited and nervous to find out exactly how far along she was and her expected due date.

Ω

The ladies made small talk while they studied their menus. Peyton couldn't resist any longer. She had to order something stronger than tea or soda.

"Please bring a bottle of your Raymond Merlot Reserve selection," she informed the server when he approached the table to take their drink orders.

"A bottle, ma'am?"

"Yes, a bottle. Do you have a problem with that?" Peyton smarted off, aggravated that the server would even ask her such a question.

"No, of course not. I just wanted to make certain, ma'am."

"I'll have an Acqua Panna water," Avery said.

"I'll have the same," added Eva.

When the server turned and left, Eva looked over at Peyton curiously.

"I thought you were laying off the alcohol," Avery said, without admitting that she couldn't drink even if she wanted to, being pregnant with Carlton's child.

"And you know I can't drink," Eva said, rubbing her slightly protruding belly in a circular motion. "So please tell me you aren't going to down a whole bottle of wine by yourself."

Peyton laughed. "Wine is to me what a soda or water is to you."

Shortly after, the server returned with the ladies' drink orders and then proceeded to take their meal orders.

"Eva, how are things going with you?" Peyton asked after the server left. She took a sip of her wine. "Hmmm. This is heavenly."

"Well, that's one of the reasons I wanted to meet you and Avery here today. I'm thinking about looking for my own place. Me and my pooches can't stay holed up in a hotel. I don't care how fancy it is, or how many amenities it has."

"So, I take it that means you and Harper haven't resolved your issues, huh?" Peyton replied. "It's a crying shame that he's acting so immature. You would think he would be excited to have a kid. I don't care how much he talked about not wanting another child."

"Yeah, I'm not feeling why he's acting like he is. There has to be more to it. Are you sure you're telling us the whole story, Eva? I mean, it's not like the man is sterile or something."

"Right," Peyton laughed while Eva lowered her head and tried to keep her tears at bay.

Avery looked over at Peyton curiously and Peyton returned the stare. The both of them then looked at Eva.

"Eva?"

Eva slowly raised her head in shame, looking at each one of her friends.

Peyton took another swallow this time from her glass of wine. Raising one finger and switching it from side to side, she said, "No, no, no. Please don't tell me what I think you're going to tell me. That man is not sterile."

"Come on, Peyton. How could he be sterile if Eva's pregnant. That would mean that—"

"That she's been bumping and grinding with somebody else," Peyton carelessly said.

Eva couldn't hold her tears back any longer. They came pouring down her cheeks.

"Peyton, you can be so darn insensitive," Avery shouted at her friend. "Don't you see the girl is troubled?"

Peyton basically ignored Avery's remark. "Is he? Is Harper sterile? Tell the truth," Peyton demanded.

Eva couldn't mouth a word. All she could do was nod her head up and down as she continued to boo-hoo.

Avery immediately opened her purse and pulled out a convenient purse size pack of tissue. She opened the pack and pushed it toward Eva.

Peyton took the last swallow of wine and poured herself another glassful. "Oh, my God. That's the reason he threw you out. I knew it had to be something far deeper than him not wanting a kid. So, tell us. Who's the baby daddy?"

Avery rolled her eyes at Peyton.

"Whaaat?" Peyton shrugged her shoulders. "If Harper is shooting blanks then our friend here was sleeping with someone else. You really pulled one over on us. I never would have thought you would step out on Harper. I mean, I can't say I blame you. Especially since you always said the man spent more nights away from home than he did at home. So who is he? Anybody we know?"

"Stop it, Peyton," Avery snapped again. "Eva, everything is going to be all right. If you don't want to tell us then don't."

Eva couldn't explain the shame she felt, but the other part of her knew that no matter how smart mouthed Peyton was that when all was said and done, she had no one else to turn to but her friends. And she could trust them, that much she was sure of.

"It's okay. I know how Peyton is," Eva said, wiping away her tears. "When I told Harper that I was pregnant, I thought he would be so thrilled. Imagine how I felt when he told me he had a vasectomy and wanted me out of the house."

Peyton and Avery's eyes seemed like they began to grow large as a full moon.

"Dang! A vasectomy. This is even juicier than I thought," Peyton said, picking up her glass of wine and taking a big gulp.

"I only slept with him once. I…I had no idea that it would lead to this. My life is ruined."

"First of all, your life is not ruined. You're not the only woman that's gotten pregnant by someone other than her man, and you won't be the last." Avery sympathized.

"Come on, who is the baby daddy?" Peyton asked again, taking yet another gulp of her wine like it was a glass of water.

"It can only be one person."

"Who?" Peyton pressured while Avery looked at Eva with pity in her eyes.

"Seth. Harper's son."

"I knew it!" Peyton almost screamed out loud enough for people at the next tables to hear.

"But I thought you said nothing happened between the two of you."

"Obviously, she lied," said Peyton.

"Won't you just please shut up, Peyton!" Avery retorted. "Just shut up already!"

Eva continued. "I lied. I was too ashamed to tell any of you. But God knows I didn't think it would lead to any of this. I just can't believe this is happening to me. I can't believe it. I can't. I can't. I can't." Eva cried harder and harder.

Avery and Peyton both got up from their seats and walked around and stood next to Eva. Each one of them embraced her.

"Come on, let's get out of here," Avery said.

"I'll take care of the check," Peyton offered. "You all meet me outside."

Avery helped Eva stand, grabbed her purse, and led a distraught Eva outside.

"I wish I had never told you to deceive Harper by getting off the pill."

"It wouldn't have mattered, Avery, seeing that the man had a vasectomy. Why did he do this to me? Why, Avery?"

"I don't know but why didn't you tell me that you slept with Seth? You know you could tell me anything."

"Like I said, I was too ashamed. It happened the day before he left to go back home to Pennsylvania. I hated myself afterward. Then Harper and I had a beautiful night together. We made love like we hadn't made love in a long time. When I missed my period the next month, to tell you the truth, I never thought for a minute that I might have gotten pregnant by Seth."

Peyton appeared and walked up next to the ladies. "Where are we going from here?" she asked.

"I...I have my first doctor's appointment this afternoon. I'm supposed to have an ultrasound scan to determine how far along I am."

"Then that's it. We're going with you," Peyton said.

"We can all ride in my car," Avery suggested. "Peyton, I don't want to hear any back talk from you. You've already had far too much to drink, so you know you're riding with me. I'll bring both of you back to pick up your cars after we leave your doctor's appointment, Eva. All right? Maybe you would have sobered up a little by then, Peyton." Avery rolled her eyes at Peyton.

Eva nodded again and allowed her friends to lead her to the car. If she had to admit anything, it was that she felt so much better having confided in them.

Chapter 4

"High expectations lead to higher disappointments."
Unknown

"Mrs. Stenberg, come on back," the nurse said.

"I want them to come with me, if that's okay,' Eva stated, looking at both Peyton and Avery.

"Sure, no problem. Come with me, ladies."

The nurse led them to the ultrasound room.

"Please get undressed and put on one of the gowns from that cubby hole," the nurse explained pointing to the cubby hole full of various sized gowns next to the table.

"Okay," Eva answered.

"The doctor will be in shortly," the nurse said and then exited the room.

Peyton sat down. The wine had her a little lightheaded, but other than that she felt she was fine.

Eva did as the nurse instructed and removed all of her clothes and put on one of the patient gowns that Avery passed her.

Avery, pregnant herself, was overly concerned because she wondered how Carlton was going to react when she told him that she was having his kid. Like Eva, she hadn't told any of the housewives. She planned on telling Eva and Peyton today but then Eva shared her sad news and Avery dismissed her plans. Plus, she wanted to tell Carlton the good news first. She hoped that he wouldn't be finished with her the same way Harper was done with Eva. Then again she dismissed that thought. Her and Carlton's relationship was different. They were very much in love. He would embrace the fact that he was going to have a kid by her.

"Hello, Mrs. Stenberg. Hello, ladies," the less than attractive young doctor said when he entered the room.

"Hello," Eva replied followed by "Hellos" from Peyton and Avery.

"So, you're pregnant? Congratulations," the doctor said.

"Thank you."

"Have you had an official pregnancy test performed?"

"No, but I've taken three at home pregnancy tests," Eva answered.

"Okay, good. But today we're going to perform an ultrasound scan. It will determine how far along you are and give us a date when the little lady or fellow will make its entrance into this mean old world," the doctor explained with a pleasant attitude and a bright smile.

He pushed a button on the wall and spoke into it. "Please send in a nurse to assist me with the ultrasound scan in Room two."

"Yes, Doctor Abbott," someone responded.

Shortly after, a nurse entered the room. "Would you like your friends to stay in here with you?" he asked.

"Yes, yes I want them here."

"Then let's get this show on the road," he said jovially.

"Mrs. Stenberg, this gel is going to be a little cold," the nurse explained.

"No problem," Eva replied.

The nurse rubbed the cold gel across Eva's belly while Peyton and Avery quietly looked on. Afterwards, the doctor stepped up and took a tool and began to rub it around Eva's belly while looking at the monitor in front of him.

He moved it around and around, not saying a word. After several minutes, he spoke up. This time his jovial smile was gone. "Mrs. Stenberg, you said you took three pregnancy tests?"

"Yes. Why? Is something wrong, doctor? Is something wrong with my baby?" Eva asked with concern resonating with each word she spoke.

Speaking slowly, he responded, "You are not pregnant."

"What? How can that be? There has to be a mistake. There just has to be."

"I don't know what to say." Avery hugged her friend. "I've never heard of this."

"Blessing in disguise if you ask me," Peyton said.

"That's it, no one asked you," Avery looked over at Peyton and rolled her eyes again.
"

"But...my belly...look at it. It's like I'm beginning to show."

"It's the cysts combined with a little wishful thinking. The mind and the way it works is a peculiar thing. Sometimes we can want something so bad, that we can manifest it."

Avery and Peyton looked at one another. Eva looked at both of them. At this moment in time, Eva didn't know if she should rejoice over the fact that she wasn't pregnant, or if she should be crying because she wasn't. What would Harper have to say after she told him this latest news? Or would she even tell him? Her mind was whirling and a thousand mixed up, confused thoughts ran through it.

"You can get dressed. I'm done for now. I'd like you to schedule an appointment with the outpatient surgery desk to remove those cysts. Once that's done, you will be relieved to know that you'll find it easier to get pregnant. So, hopefully, that's good news for you," Doctor Abbott said with empathy. "You ladies have a good evening." He walked out of the room and closed the door behind him.

"Let me get this gel off of you, then you can get dressed," the nurse said, getting a towel from inside the table drawer and using it to wipe Eva's belly clean.

The three friends exited the doctor's office and headed back to Avery's car. They got in the car and sat in the parking lot for several minutes talking.

"Are you okay?" Avery spoke up first.

"I don't know whether to be relieved or disappointed. I still don't understand how I got three positive test results and not be pregnant. I just don't get it."

"I've heard of this sort of thing before," Peyton answered.

"You have?" Eva looked at Peyton like she wanted to hear more.

"Yes. Of course, it was on one of those reality shows. But, still, the girl on there did just like you. She took two or three pregnancy tests and they all came out positive. She told her boyfriend about it and everything. When she made an appointment to go see her gynecologist, they did the same thing they did to you, take a ultrasound scan."

"And?" said Avery. "What happened?"

"It was just like Eva's doctor told her. The woman wasn't pregnant. She had cysts and the doctor told her that it's more common than we hear of to get false positives from pregnancy tests. The woman was heartbroken. But then within three months, she was pregnant, and this time it was for real. In your case, and this is not to sound insensitive, but this really may be a blessing in disguise." Peyton looked at Avery expecting her to say something against her again.

"I hate to say it, but now that I think about it, I guess I agree with you, Peyton. This really could be a blessing, Eva. God revealed that your husband had been lying to you all along. I can't believe Harper would do such a thing. Maybe it took something like this to happen for you to see him for the kind of man he really is. I mean, there was no reason whatsoever for him to withhold that he had a vasectomy. No reason at all."

"I don't know why he would do me like that."

"And no one ever has to know that you slept with Seth."

"What?! You slept with Harper's kid? Oh, no you didn't," Peyton burst out.

Avery quickly placed her hand over her mouth. "Oops, I'm sorry. I forgot that Peyton wasn't outside with us when you told me. I'm so sorry, Eva. Me and my big mouth."

"You little freak," Peyton squealed, bouncing back and forth against the back seat.

"This is between us," said Avery. "Don't you dare tell a soul."

"Come on, now. I may joke around with you all a lot, but you should know that I'm not one to tell anyone outside of our circle what we talk about. I got you, Eva. Actually, it's good to know that you aren't a stuck up prude like I pegged you to be." Peyton chuckled.

Eva smiled lightly. "I love you ladies. Thank you for coming with me today and being by my side."

"We wouldn't have it any other way. I just wish Meesha had been here, too," Peyton said.

Avery didn't respond.

"Yeah, me, too. I hope things are going okay with her. Have either of you heard from her?"

"No, I haven't. She won't return my calls or texts. She still thinks I slept with Carlton, which couldn't be further from the truth. And even if I did, look how long ago that was. Liam is going on fifteen. It's not like he's a newborn baby, for Christ's sake. I wish she would let sleeping dogs lie."

"Have you heard anything from Derek and Liam about them coming back home?"

"I talked to Liam. He doesn't want to see me, but what can I expect? It's a lot for him to digest. To find out through the news media that I'm not his birth mother and that the woman who *is* his mother was a junkie, and now she's dead without him ever getting a chance to know her for himself.

"Wow, I can't imagine what he's thinking," Eva said. "And here I am wallowing in self-pity when that poor child has been left confused and hurt. And I'm not blaming you, Peyton. You saved Liam's life. He may be too young and too hurt to realize that now, but it's the truth."

"Yeah, she's right, Peyton. Only God knows where he would be, or if he would even be alive, if you hadn't stepped in. He's blessed to have you for a mother. You and Derek have been nothing but good to him."

"Thanks." Peyton's own eyes welled up with tears. "I just pray that Liam will forgive me. Derek too. I didn't mean for anything like this to happen. And Breyonna is dead; that's awful. I don't care how much havoc she wreaked in my life and Carlton's, she didn't deserve to die like she did."

"Do you think Derek will ever forgive you?"

"I don't know, but what I can tell you is that if I ever expect to have a chance to get my family back, I have some changes to make."

"Your drinking?" Avery asked.

"Yes. I've got to stop it altogether. I know I have a problem. But drinking helps me cope. I know it's not good for me, but, well anyway, I'm going to stop. This time I mean it."

"You can do it. All you have to do is ask God for help. He'll come through for you," Avery said.

Peyton looked over at Avery and smiled. "You sound like Meesha."

Eva laughed lightly. "You sure do. You sound just like a First Lady."

Avery half smiled while thinking to herself. *I can't wait to be Carlton's first lady.*

Chapter 5

"Once a woman has forgiven her man, she must not reheat his sins for breakfast." Marlene Dietrich

Meesha and the boys walked into the house. The boys took off toward their rooms as soon as they stepped inside. Meesha took a moment and stood inside the foyer. Was she ready to face Carlton? Had she made a mistake by coming home?

She exhaled and walked further into the house. She went up the spiraling staircase and headed to the bedroom, a bedroom that used to mean peace and love, but now held lies and deceit inside its walls. As she opened the door, a sweet fragrance wafted through her nostrils. She pressed the button on the wall as she entered the room, and the lights came on. Her eyes widened when she took in the view of beautiful, fresh roses and tulips of all colors and in some of the most exquisite looking vases she'd ever seen. The sight almost took her breath away. She walked closer, leaned in, and inhaled the sweet, tantalizing fragrances.

For a moment, life felt normal. This was the kind of thing Carlton was known for. He often surprised her with flowers, something he knew she loved. And roses and tulips were her favorite. She continued to walk around and sniff the vases of flowers. On the bed, she noticed an envelope. She sauntered over to the bed, picked it up, and opened it. Inside was a card. *"Welcome home, my love. I have so much wrong to right. I hope you will give me the chance to make it up to you. I love you more than you can ever imagine. Thank you for coming home to me. Hope these roses and tulips let you know what you mean to me. Carlton."*

Meesha smiled, although she remained full of hurt. She always readily told others about how important it was to forgive but now that she faced a situation in her own marriage, it was hard to take her own advice. Another thing she would tell married couples and couples who planned to marry was that it was essential that they communicated. Again, she wouldn't listen to Carlton. She didn't want to hear anything he had to say. Now she understood how wrong she had been. Whether she believed him or not, that was not the issue. The issue was that Carlton kept trying, kept reaching out to her, and she refused every single time. But she was hurt. Hurt that he could possibly have cheated on her with Peyton.

The house phone rang. It had to be Carlton. No one called that phone but him, her, or their sons. She walked over to the phone located next to their California king bed. She picked it up from its cradle, pressed the button and spoke into it.

"Hello."

"Welcome home, Meesha. I hope you and the boys had a good flight."

"We did," she responded. "The flowers are beautiful. My favorite. But how did you know when we would arrive or that we were coming home?"

"I'm glad you like them, and to answer your questions, CJ texted me and told me that you all were coming home today. I called Geena after that and she told me what time your flight was supposed to arrive."

Silence temporarily filled the phone space between them.

"Where are the boys? I suspect that they're in their rooms." Carlton laughed.

It sounded good to hear him laugh. Meesha loved the sound of his laughter. It always made her feel safe and secure.

"You know it. We barely stepped foot in the house and off they went. I haven't seen or heard them since."

"How long have you been there?"

"Only about ten minutes or so."

"I really wish you had let me pick you and the boys up from the airport."

"I needed to do this. I just wasn't ready to see you."

"And now?"

"And now what?" she asked.

"Do you think we can take some time to sit down and talk?"

"I think that would be good. I have some news to share."

"Good news I hope?"

"I don't know. I'll let you be the judge of that. But first I want to hear what you have to say."

"What about dinner?" Carlton asked, cautiously.

"With me and the boys?"

"Yes, I wouldn't have it any other way. And afterwards, we can talk, alone."

"Sure."

"I was thinking we could take the boys out for pizza. I think they'd enjoy that."

"I know they will. They miss their father."

"Thanks for letting me know that."

"That's something I shouldn't have to tell you. You know how much they love you."

"And their mother?"

"Carlton, I never stopped loving you." Meesha walked around the room as she talked, still taking in the array of flowers and inhaling the sweetness of their scent. "I just didn't know if you stopped loving me."

"I'll send a car to pick up you and the boys. How does seven-thirty sound?"

Meesha hoped he would say the words "I love you" in return, but he didn't. That was the issue she had about everything that had happened. Had Carlton stopped loving her?

"Seven-thirty will be fine. We'll see you tonight." She pushed the OFF button on the phone and laid it down on the dresser.

Her oldest son walked into the room. "Wow, look at all these flowers. Looks like somebody's funeral," CJ said.

"Not now, CJ," she said agitated.

"I was just kidding. Mom, I'm hungry."

"I just talked to your father. He's going to take us out for pizza later this evening. You can grab a snack until then. I'm sure there's plenty of food in the fridge and the cabinets."

"Yes, ma'am."

"Tell your brothers, too. And, CJ, I want you all to take showers and change clothes after you eat something."

"Yes, ma'am," CJ answered, and ran out of the room.

Meesha sat down on the bed, then climbed up in it and laid down. She looked over at Carlton's side of the bed and imagined him there. She missed him. Missed the scent of him. Missed the touch of him. She missed everything about him.

"God, if it is your will, heal my marriage. Help me to listen to what Carlton has to say tonight without prejudging him. Give me a heart to forgive. Direct me, guide me, show me what you want me to do. I want my marriage, Father God. I want my husband. But most of all, I want your will, Lord."

Meesha laid in silence then leaned over and removed a red rose from one of the vases. She laid back on the bed, breathing in its intoxicating aroma.

Her cell phone text notifier chimed, coming between her and thoughts of what Carlton would have to say when she told him that she was pregnant with baby number five.

"When   r u coming home?" the text from Eva read.

"Made it back a while ago."

"Oh, u didn't say u were coming, but glad ur back."

"HRU?" Meesha texted back.

"OK. Got some news today need to share w u. we'll talk ltr."

"Will call u soon. Going to meet Carlton for dinner ltr. Me n the boys."

"K. just call me when u hve some time."

"Going to shower I'll call u when I'm done," Meesha replied.

"k. ttyl," Eva answered.

Chapter 6

"There is always some madness in love. But there is also always some reason in madness." Friedrich Nietzsche

Avery nervously paced across the dark hardwood floors of her home. Tonight she planned on telling Carlton that she was pregnant. But after seeing how things turned out with Eva, she was a little uneasy about sharing the news. Maybe she should go see her gynecologist first to make sure she was really pregnant. If Eva could have a false positive pregnancy result, maybe the same thing could happen to her.

"Mom," Lexie called, as she entered the family room where Avery was.

"What is it, Lexie?"

"Can I spend the night with Ruby?"

"Honey, I don't think so. I haven't talked to Ruby's mom about it. Maybe another time, okay?"

"But, Mom, I want to stay tonight," Lexie pleaded.

"What did I just say? It's too late. Where is Heather?"

Lexie pouted. "In her room."

"Okay, good. When your father gets here, maybe we'll go out for pizza."

Lexie's pout changed into a smile. "Yayyyy, pizza. Can I order the kind of pizza that I want, Mom?"

"We'll see. Now go tell your sister that we're going for pizza. I want both of you to change into some other clothes. Okay?"

"Okay." Lexie ran out of the family room, leaving Avery alone with her thoughts about what the future held for her. Ryker had asked to marry her after all of the years they'd been together. The only thing about that was that she didn't think she wanted him anymore. She wanted a new life with Carlton. Carlton made her feel like she was important, like she mattered. Ryker had done just the opposite. He had taken her love for granted and after giving him two beautiful and precious little girls, he still didn't value her. Him sleeping with her cousin was what did it for her. He tried to make her believe that his infidelity had been her fault, but after being counselled by Carlton, she came to understand that no one can make you feel inferior without your consent. When Carlton told her that, she made up in her mind never to let Ryker or anyone make her feel that she was less than. Never again would she try to end her life.

"Thank you, Lord," she said quietly as she stopped pacing and went outside and sat on the lanai. "Thank you for keeping me alive. How could I try to end my life when I have two precious little girls that need me and love me? How could I? Please forgive me," she prayed.

Her thoughts switched back to her present dilemma. Supposed this wasn't Carlton's baby in her belly. It was possible that it could be Ryker's child inside of her, but she doubted it. She and Ryker had made love weeks before her and Carlton first made love, and since then she refused Ryker's sexual advances as often as she could without upsetting him.

"I better make an appointment to see my doctor," she said, talking to herself. She got up and went to the office located on the first floor of their three story red brick home. She opened the French doors leading into the office and went inside. At the computer, she logged onto her doctor's website and went to the tab where it said APPOINTMENTS. She proceeded to schedule an appointment. Just as she closed the tab, she heard someone enter the office. Looking up and around, she met eyes with Ryker.

"Hey, what you doing?" he asked, walking over to her.

"Oh, nothing. Just browsing the internet and looking at my social media page."

"I see." He kissed her on top of her head. "How was your day?"

"Quite eventful to say the least."

"Oh? Why is that?"

"Me and the girls had lunch at Zodiac Cafe then me and Peyton went with Eva to her doctor's appointment."

"How is she?"

"I don't know if I should tell you. After all, you're the one that referred Harper to that attorney friend of yours."

"Business is business. You should know that. It's nothing against Eva. Harper asked me to refer him to a divorce attorney and that's what I did. What did you expect?"

Avery shrugged her shoulders, turned around in the deep cushioned office chair, and proceeded to stand up. "You're right. I can't blame you."

"So, how is she?"

"She's not pregnant."

"What?"

"The doctor said she had false positives on her pregnancy test. He performed an ultrasound scan and it showed that she wasn't pregnant after all. She has some cysts that he suggested she have removed."

"She should be glad about that. Maybe she and Harper can mend their relationship now."

"I don't know. She may not want to. Especially after the way Harper treated her."

"Do you blame him?"

"I know you don't want me to answer that."

"Why wouldn't I?" Ryker said. He sat down on the edge of the oak office desk, folded his arms, and waited on her reply.

"Let's just say that you aren't exactly one to talk. I forgave you for cheating on me, yet you treat me like I'm the one that slept around. But I don't want to talk about that. What's done is done."

"Neither do I. It's like beating a dead horse. I made a mistake. I asked you to forgive me. You said that you did. So it's done. Over with." Ryker tried to remain calm. He didn't feel like arguing, he wanted to do what he could to make things work between him and Avery.

"Whatever, Ryker. Anyway, I told the girls that we would all go out for pizza when you got home."

"Okay, that's cool. I'm going to go say hi to them, take a shower, and we can leave around seven or seven thirty. How's that?"

"Sounds good."

Ryker left out of the office and went upstairs. He went to Lexie and Heather's room and played with them before going to his and Avery's bedroom to take a shower. He didn't know how much longer his relationship could or would survive. Ever since Avery's failed suicide attempt, things had been different. He liked that she acted more confident and sure of herself.

What he didn't like was the lackadaisical way she treated him and their relationship. He blamed himself for not making her his wife. He didn't know if deep down inside he felt like she wasn't wife material. After all, when they first met, she was a high priced call girl and an exotic dancer. But was it her fault that he fell in love with her? He knew what and who she was before he became involved with her and yet when he ran back into her in Florida, he pursued a relationship with her. He had to admit that she changed her life around but there was still part of him that possibly punished her for her past life.

They were faithful members of Perfecting Your Faith and Ryker clung to his faith, hoping that he would become a better man. After Avery survived the suicide attempt, he set out to prove to her that she was special to him and that he loved her, because he did love her. He had made up in his mind that he wanted her to marry him, but she had refused on more than one occasion. That troubled him because there was a time when marriage was all Avery wanted from him. Now that he was ready to take that step, she had backed all the way off, but he refused to pressure her about it.

He stood under the hot jets of water and took a long shower, hoping somehow that the uneasy thoughts that saturated his mind would also be washed away.

Avery came upstairs, checked in on the girls to make sure they had changed clothes like she told them, and then went into the bedroom. Ryker was still in the shower. She went to an adjacent area of the master bedroom, separated by a barn type door. Inside was a space designated just for her. Her own woman cave. She smiled as she pushed the door to the side and entered the room. Ryker had his own man cave on the top floor complete with a game room, media room, and lounge. Her space was small, intimate, and just for her. She reveled in the peace and tranquility she was able to find inside that room. She went over and sat in one of the high back chairs in the far east corner of the room. It was a space where she often relaxed, read a book, or listened to some of her favorite music.

She gathered up both legs and sat Indian style in the chair, laid her head back, and thought about when and how she would tell Ryker that she wanted out of their relationship. She would have to be extra careful. With Ryker being a highly successful lawyer, representing celebrities and sports athletes alike, she knew the first thing he would probably set out to do was to get full custody of the girls. That was her major concern and the reason she had to handle things carefully. Somehow, she would have to find a lawyer that wouldn't divulge to Ryker what her plans were. Not until she was good and ready. Maybe Carlton would be able to recommend someone.

She heard Ryker shuffling around in the bedroom. She went to the door and saw him standing at the chest of drawers with a towel wrapped around his glistening wet body. Ryker took good care of himself. His chocolate skin was smooth as a baby's bottom. His naturally thick straight hair revealed his Indian heritage. Before he cut it, it used to come down to the middle of his back. Now he wore it cut close to his scalp. It accentuated his blackness and made him all the more handsome and sexy. It's funny how the very thing that used to turn her on, now did nothing for her. He was still a good looking man, but in her eyes he couldn't hold a candle to Carlton Porter. Carlton wasn't half as attractive as Ryker, but when a woman's heart shifted away from a man she once loved and adored, there was nothing that he could say or do to make her feel the way she once had.

Unfortunately, that's what had happened with her. Ryker had hurt her too much and too deeply. No matter how good the love making used to be, it did nothing for her now. No matter how his kisses, or his look, used to set her on fire, it did nothing to her now. The blaze was gone and now only Carlton Porter could light it.

Chapter 7

*"When an inner situation is not made conscious,
it appears outside as fate."* Carl Jung

"I want cheese pizza," Lexie said.

"I want pepperoni and sausage," Heather chimed in.

"What about we order one of each," Ryker told his daughters.

"What do you girls think about that?" Avery asked.

"Okay, two pizzas." Lexie and Heather replied.

Ryker went to order the two pizzas plus a salad for Avery.

Talking to her daughters and texting Eva at the same time, Avery looked up and saw Meesha, Carlton, and their four sons walking into the popular restaurant.

When did she get back in town? Avery said to herself. *And why are they together? I thought their marriage was over.* Carlton hadn't given her any indication or reason to think that he and Meesha were going to try and salvage their marriage.

Carlton walked in, his hand went to the small of Meesha's back. It was the same term of endearment he often showed her. Avery couldn't help it. A twinge of jealousy mounted inside of her at the sight of them. They were laughing and talking like they were still the perfect family.

Meesha looked up and over in her direction. She whispered something in Carlton's ear and then walked away from him, coming in her direction.

"Hey, girl," Meesha said as she approached Avery's table. She bent over and hugged Avery. "Hi, girls," she said to Lexie and Heather.

"Hey, welcome back," Avery said, returning the hug and trying to sound as happy as she could. "When did you get back into town?"

"Earlier today."

"Oh, I see." She looked at the front where Carlton and his boys were. She watched them out of the corner of her eye as they went toward a large table and sat down with menus in hand.

"How have you been?" Meesha asked.

"I'm good. I'm sort of surprised to see you back. Have things changed between you and Carlton?"

"Not really. But it's not the place or time to talk about that. Have you seen or talked to Peyton? Not that I have anything to say to her. I heard from Eva when I first got back."

"Yeah, the three of us had lunch today at Zodiac Café. I'm sure you'll hear all about it later. It was quite an interesting day. That's all I can say for now," Avery remarked, looking at Meesha then at Lexie and Heather.

"I understand. I can't wait. Eva texted me earlier when I first got home. I was supposed to call her back but got wrapped up with some other stuff. You know how it is when you've been away from home on a trip. Things have to get done."

Ryker walked up. "Hello, Meesha." He leaned in to hug her but Meesha stepped back.

"Hi, Ryker," she said coldly. "We'll talk later, Avery," Meesha said and promptly walked off.

"Guess I know how she feels about me. No sense in having her lips on swoll just because I referred Carlton to the best divorce lawyer in this city, hell, in this state. I did the same for Harper, but I don't guess Eva is whining about it." Ryker grinned. "Hey, but it is what it is."

Avery shrugged it off. Her mind was on other things. Like what was up with Carlton and Meesha.

Meesha crossed the busy pizza and game room floor. She sat down at the table with her family. "Have you guys decided what to order?"

"I know what you want," Carlton said. "The veggie pizza, no cheese, extra marinara sauce and loads of vegetables."

"You got it," she said.

"I see Avery over there with her family," Carlton observed. He locked eyes with Avery for a few seconds, then quickly shifted his gaze. Today was the day that he was supposed to tell her that things were done and over. He hadn't. He had put it off, but knew that the longer he did, the harder it would be – on her. It threw him for a loop when he learned Meesha was coming home, so the last thing on his mind was meeting up with Avery.

The more Carlton thought about the situation and prayed over it, the more he understood the huge error of his ways. He was glad that he'd talked to his brother. Kingston helped him see that he had totally crossed the line. He was a man of God. He was supposed to be a person people could trust, confide in, yet, he felt he had taken advantage of Avery when she was at a low point in her life.

"Yeah, I went over there and spoke," Meesha said, intruding on Carlton's thoughts. "I'm glad I got a chance to see her. She looks good. Ryker, on the other hand, let's just say I have very little to say to him."

"Meesha, really, it's no sense in taking things out on Ryker. He did what Harper asked him to do. Plus, that's between Harper and Eva." Meesha had no idea that Carlton had also talked to Ryker about recommending a good divorce attorney, and he referred him to the same fellow that he had referred Harper to.

"You're one to talk."

"Come on, babe. Let's not do this. We're here to have family time. I've missed you and my sons." He looked at his boys who were busy talking to each other. "Can we go play some video games?" one of the boys asked.

"Sure. You think I brought you here just to eat pizza? We can't leave until I beat you guys at basketball."

"You can't beat us," Marlon rebelled.

"He's right, Dad." Malik said.

"Okay, tell you what. Here are the tokens I bought when we came in. Go have a good time. I'll join you later when you're ready for me to come beat you at basketball," he teased.

"In your dreams," CJ said and all of them laughed, including Meesha.

This was what she loved, spending time and hanging out with her family. Carlton was always a good father. If Liam really was his son, and they miraculously stayed together, she would have to find a way to blend him in with their family. It would take a lot of prayer, and she didn't know if she would be able to do it in and of herself. It could only work out with God's help.

She and Carlton watched the boys run off toward the bevy of video games inside the pizza place.

"Do you want me to go up and order the pizza or would you rather I wait until a server comes?"

"Doesn't matter to me," Meesha answered.

"Then I'll wait on a server," Carlton replied.

Meesha shrugged.

"Look, Meesha. I know I've put you through a lot lately. Telling you that I wanted a divorce, then all of this stuff with Peyton and Liam. I can't imagine what you must be thinking. But I'm sorry."

Meesha remained silent. She clasped her hands together and rested her chin on them with her elbows on the table.

The server walked up. "Are you ready to place your order?" the pleasant young woman asked.

"Yes. I'll have one medium veggie pizza, heavy on the vegetables but no cheese and with extra marinara sauce, one medium cheese pizza, and a large pepperoni and sausage."

"Will that be all?"

"Oh, a family size order of fries. We'll wait on the drink refills until our order comes back."

"Okay, I'll put your order in now. Thank you," she said and left their table.

"I still can't do the vegan thing," he said, looking at Meesha.

"That's totally on you."

"Meesha," he said, getting serious. "I have never had an affair or messed off with Peyton. We were friends back in college, but you already know that. As far as Liam, I promise you, I didn't know the circumstances surrounding him and Peyton. I knew that I might possibly have a kid out there somewhere because on one occasion years ago, when Liam would have been a toddler, I ran into Breyonna, and she told me I had a kid. I didn't take her serious because the woman was a dope fiend. She asked me for money and I gave it to her, but I never saw a kid. Then when she showed up here in Adverse City, I didn't know what to do. I learned later that she contacted Peyton threatening her and telling her she wanted Liam back. She told Peyton that I was Liam's father."

"And are you?" Meesha asked coldly.

"I don't know. I honestly don't."

"Then why are you so willing to accept him as your son if you aren't sure?"

Carlton paused in thought. He glanced in the direction of where Avery and her family were seated. Again, their eyes locked.

"Because," he said, reverting his attention back to Meesha's question. "Because he has a birthmark almost identical to mine and in the same place as mine. How likely is that?"

"I don't know. It's not like you have a lockdown on birthmarks," Meesha replied smugly.

"True, but you asked me why I was willing to say that he was my son and that's the reason why. But I'm going to have a DNA test to find out once and for all if he is my son. Regardless, I want things to work out between you and me, Meesha."

"I don't understand you, Carlton. You've been telling me for months that you want a divorce, that you no longer wanted to be married. Now you're sitting across the table from me telling me that you've suddenly had a change of heart, and you expect me to come running back?"

"I know it's a lot to ask. But I'm telling you, sweetheart that I ran scared when Breyonna came to town. I didn't want to embarrass you so I thought before the media got wind of what was going on, the best thing to do was to divorce you. I wanted to be the bad guy because I *was* the bad guy. I don't know how else to explain it. All I'm asking you to do is pray about it. Pray and ask God to show you what to do concerning our marriage," Carlton begged.

"Did you think to pray before you asked me for a divorce, Carlton? Did you think to come and talk to me, to tell me the truth. My God, it's not like you're having an affair now. We're talking about a child that's fifteen years old!"

Carlton swallowed hard. He was not about to confess to having an affair with Avery. No way. But Meesha's word gave him pause. A stab of fresh guilt pricked at his heart.

"I guess I didn't. I didn't trust God enough to give me the answer. I know that may sound funny, me being in the position I'm in with the church and all, but the human part of me ran scared. And again, I don't know what else to say other than I'm sorry. I want my family back. I want you back, Meesha. I want my boys back. Please, baby. Please tell me that you'll forgive me."

Meesha's eyes filled with tears. She didn't want to cry. She wanted to be strong. She wanted to hate Carlton, but she couldn't. This was the man that she loved. She fell in love with him the first time their eyes met and she'd loved him ever since. But he'd hurt her so badly and she didn't know if she could be able to forgive him. She desperately wanted to, but the wounded part of her wouldn't allow her to fully release Carlton to come back into her life. It would definitely take God.

"Carlton, one thing you said that I agree with and that is we have to trust God. I want our family and our marriage to work. But this pain, this pain runs deep. Yet, I know God is able. And, well, all I can promise you is that I'll try. I have no choice since I'm carrying your child."

Carlton was totally taken aback. "What did you say?" he said, a huge smile appearing on his face. "Did you say you're carrying my baby?"

From across the restaurant, Avery watched. Ryker and the girls were away from the table playing video games, leaving her alone with a good view of Carlton. She saw the huge smile form on his face and wondered what Meesha had said. Had she told him she wanted to save their marriage? *Well, no such luck,* Avery thought to herself. *He's mine, all mine now.*

Meesha nodded, "Yes, I'm pregnant." For the first time in a long time, Meesha allowed herself to smile then she broke out in a chuckle. "We're pregnant," she beamed.

"What? If this isn't God," Carlton said, jumping up from his chair and running to his wife's side of the table and pulling her chair back.

"Carlton, what are you doing?" she asked, taken by pleasant surprise.

He scooped her up in his arms and twirled her round and round right in the restaurant. "You're carrying my baby," he all but yelled.

Avery basically read his lips. The restaurant was too loud for her to actually hear what he was saying.

"We're pregnant. Thank you, God. Thank you, God," he said louder and louder.

There was no mistaking his words this time around because Avery had gotten up from her seat and walked over to Carlton and Meesha's table, just as he said the words out loud.

"Pregnant? Oh, baby. That's fantastic news."

"Avery, hi. What are you doing here?" Carlton stopped and said, surprised to see that Avery had walked up on them.

"Did I hear you say that you're pregnant?" Avery asked trying to hide the indignation in her voice.

"Yes. You heard right. I'm pregnant," Meesha confessed, holding her belly, while Carlton looked on nervously, uncertain if Avery would say something and ruin everything.

"God acts in mysterious ways," Meesha said.

"He most certainly does." Avery said and started walking off. "Oh, by the way, congratulations. I'll talk to you some other time, Meesha," Avery said coolly.

With a curious look on her face, Meesha watched as Avery swiftly walked away.

Chapter 8

"It is a lonely feeling when someone you care about becomes a stranger." Unknown

The following morning, Peyton got up early. The bright Florida sun made her feel especially hopeful. She had a difficult task ahead but she told herself that Derek would hear her out. All she wanted was to get the DNA test done and over with.

She showered, and got dressed, choosing an ankle length designer sundress and heels. She sprayed on a dash of her favorite perfume, then went downstairs to enjoy a breakfast of a toasted bagel and a strong black cup of coffee.

After breakfast, she called Derek. He picked up right away.

"What is it, Peyton."

"Hello to you too," she remarked. She was getting sick of his holier than thou attitude toward her. He acted like he was so perfect when in reality he was far from it. He'd done his share of things during their marriage that could have taken them directly past go and straight into divorce court, but yet, she'd stuck it out with him. She hardly ever told him that she loved him, but truth be told, she really did. He was a good man. He was a good father, and he was most definitely a good provider. Sure, her parents helped him out when they first started out, and she was the one with the money, but he'd earned his own way now, and made his own fortune apart from her money. He was a go getter, a hustler, and it had paid off handsomely for him and for them as a family.

"I want to talk to you," she told him, dispelling her thoughts and feelings toward him and instead focusing on the present situation.

"I'm at the office, so talk quick. I have a meeting in ten minutes."

"When will you be free? I want to come to the office or meet you for lunch."

"I don't know."

"If you want me to beg, then okay, I'll beg. Please, Derek. This is important. It's about Liam."

Silence.

"Meet me at Zuma at eleven."

"I'll be there."

"Goodbye, Peyton. Oh, and one more thing," he added.

"What is it?"

"Please be sober."

"I'll see you at eleven," Peyton said, ashamed that her husband would have to request such a thing of her.

She had to change things in her life. If there was ever a chance of getting her husband and son to come back home, she would have to do something drastic, and she knew exactly what that was. Once she got things settled with the DNA test and got the results, she was going to enter rehab. She pulled out her phone from the hidden pocket on her sundress, and searched the number of the best Drug and Alcohol center in the country.

"Hi, can you send me some information on your program, please."

Ω

Sitting across the table from Derek, she stared into his deep dark brown eyes. He had always been a handsome man to Peyton. He was tall, stocky, coffee cream complexion, and in her eyes nothing short of a genius.

He'd taken a hard knock life and turned it into multimillionaire status. He was driven and assertive, all turn-ons to Peyton.

"So you say you want Liam to have a DNA test?"

"Yes, I do. I've got to talk to Carlton, but I'm sure he'll agree. Breyonna is dead, God rest her soul. And Liam will never know her. I can't say that I'm sad about that part. The woman would have ruined his life, but of course I didn't want her dead."

"You sure about that?" Derek said sarcastically."

"I'm not going to let you make me go there, Derek. I want Liam to know for sure if Carlton is his father. If he is, then I'll let Liam decide if he wants a relationship with him."

"And what about you, Peyton?"

"What do you mean?"

"Are you going to leave it up to him to decide if he still wants a relationship with you?"

His question stung. It was so unexpected. She couldn't fathom not having a relationship with her son. She loved Liam. He kept her going. He kept her alive and he made her want to do better. Maybe he wouldn't want to have anything to do with her now, and she could understand that. He was hurt and angry. It was a lot for a fifteen year old kid to digest. But she was going to do whatever it took to right things for him.

"I can say this, I hope he forgives me, and I hope you forgive me as well. I want my marriage to work. I want us to be a family again. I haven't told you this since God knows when, but I'm going to tell you now."

"Tell me what?"

"That I love you."

Derek appeared shocked. Hearing Peyton confess love for him surprisingly tugged at his heart, making him feel some type of way. He'd long accepted the fact that his marriage only existed for the sake of Liam. Peyton's heavy drinking had caused such a huge rift in what used to be to Derek, the perfect relationship. Isn't that how most marriages begin? Starry eyed lovers, thinking, hoping, and believing that the love they first saw in each other will last forever. Doesn't every married couple enter marriage believing in happily ever after? Derek had to soon come to the raw realization that that wasn't what real life was all about. The light in his life was his son. He adopted Liam and no matter what a DNA test proved, he would forever be Liam's father.

"You love me. That's a joke, Peyton."

"I'm serious, Derek. I love you."

"Look, I have to get back to the office in about forty-five minutes, so let's get to the real reason you wanted me here."

"I want you to come back home. I want you and our son back. I'm willing to do whatever it takes to make that happen."

"Meaning what?" Derek responded nonchalantly. It was hard to believe anything Peyton said. She'd promised time and time again to stop the drinking, but yet it only got worse instead of better. This huge reveal about Liam and this dead woman who claimed she was his birth mother, only made him realize that Peyton couldn't be trusted. Now she was sitting across the table from him confessing undying love for him, promising that once again she would change, and he just did not believe a word coming out of her mouth.

"Derek, I want this DNA test done. No matter what the results turn out to be, you and I both know that Liam is your son. You adopted him. You've raised him and he loves you. You're his father no matter what a DNA test says. After the results come back, I'm going into rehab."

Derek stopped eating his food. He laughed so loud that Peyton looked around to see if anyone else noticed. She was embarrassed and ashamed. "You have got to be kidding me. I know you do not expect me to believe that. You? And rehab? That's a joke if I ever heard one." Derek said and continued chuckling.

"I mean it, Derek. I've already checked into it. I've called them and made arrangements to visit the facility next week. I don't care if you believe me or not, and I can't say that I blame you for not believing me. But I'm serious this time. I realize I have too much at stake. If it means I need to go away to get myself together, then I'm going to do it. I'm just asking you to keep doing what you're doing and that's looking after our son."

"I'll never stop doing that. I don't care what some dang DNA test says or doesn't say. As for you going to rehab, I'll believe it when I see it. I can't promise you anything, Peyton. I can't say that me and Liam will be waiting for you with open arms. You haven't gone anywhere yet, and frankly I don't think you will. You'll go back to your old ways. Tell me, when was the last time you had a drink? If you've really changed, you'll tell the truth." Derek eyed her, not once deflecting his stare.

It made Peyton a little uneasy, but she accepted his stare, looked back at him, and spoke the truth. Yesterday," she said.

"Exactly what I thought. At least you were honest. I guess. You sure you didn't have some coffee with your morning cup of vodka," he mocked.

"No, I didn't. And I deserve your sarcasm but you just watch what I tell you."

Derek picked up his cloth napkin, wiped his mouth, and backed away from the table. "I've got to get back to the office." He saw the server and beckoned for him to come over. "Will you please bring the check?"

"Yes, sir," the man said.

"For Liam's sake, I hope you're telling the truth this time, Peyton. As for you and me, I can't promise you what will happen between us."

"That's fair enough," Peyton answered, although it wasn't exactly what she wanted to hear about the future of their relationship.

The server returned with the check. "Here you go, Sir."

"Thanks." Derek placed his American Express card inside the black holder along with a comparable tip for the seventy-six dollar meal.

The server returned shortly after with Derek's card and receipt.

Derek stood up. "Call or text me when the DNA test is scheduled. I'll make sure Liam is there. Have yourself a good day, Peyton." He paused before walking off. Looking at his wife for the first time with softness in his eyes, he said, "I really do hope and pray that you mean what you say. It would be a shame to lose everything we've tried to build for Liam all these years...and for us."

Peyton left the restaurant more determined than ever to change her life situation. She got in her car and called Carlton. He didn't pick up so she texted him. "Scheduling a DNA test for you and Liam. Will let u know date/time."

As she put the car in drive she called to check up on Eva. She hadn't heard from her or Avery since they met for lunch a couple of days ago. She wondered if Eva had talked to Harper and told him that she wasn't pregnant.

"Hey, girl. How are things going?" she asked Eva. Eva's three Yorkies were barking loudly in the background.

"Shush," she said and almost immediately everything went quiet. "I'm okay. What are you doing today?"

"I just left from having lunch with Derek."

"Oh, yeah. How did that go?"

"Umm, as well as can be expected. I told him about having a DNA test done."

"What'd he say about that?"

"Nothing much. Like we both agreed, he'll always be Liam's father. Nothing or no one can take that away from him."

"Well, that's true. And what about you and him? Do you see the two of you getting back together?"

"I hope so. I told him once this DNA test is done and we know who Liam's biological father is, then I'm checking myself into rehab."

"Are you serious?" Eva asked, surprised to hear Peyton say this.

"As a heart attack," was Peyton's response. "I want my family back. That means I have to make some serious changes, starting with my out of control drinking."

"You don't know how happy I am to hear you say that, Peyton. I'm behind you one hundred percent. I know Avery will be too, and whether you believe it or not, so will Meesha. You know she's back in town, don't you?" Eva told her.

"No, I didn't. And thanks for being such a good friend. I know I've said and done some things way out of line. That's with all of you, and I'm sorry. I really am."

"I know you are. Half of the time, we just chalk it up to you being Peyton, or you being wasted," Eva laughed lightly into the phone. "But seriously, I think you should reach out to Meesha one more time. Who knows, maybe she'll listen to you this time around."

"I might just do that. So what does the remainder of your day look like?" Peyton asked.

"I haven't gone to see Harper yet nor have I tried to call him. I need some time to myself to digest this. I still can't believe that I'm not pregnant. My belly was swelling and everything. I had morning sickness. I wonder if the doctor is wrong."

"You heard what he said. You're not pregnant, Eva. I know it's hard for you to accept. You wanted babies so badly, and I understand that. And I believe you're going to have a kid, but you're not pregnant. Have you scheduled the appointment to see about getting the cysts removed? The doctor said it would be outpatient surgery, and I'll be more than happy to go with you."

"Yes, the scheduling nurse is supposed to be calling me back with my appointment. I'll let you know. As for today, I was thinking about going out to look for a house or condo to move into. I'm tired of hotel living. And my babies don't have the freedom they need here. I've got to get something of my own."

"Is Harper still footing all expenses?"

"Yeah."

"And you haven't talked to him at all?"

"No, not really."

"I'm not trying to be funny when I ask you this, but have you talked to Seth?"

Eva immediately felt a little irritated. Not over the fact Peyton asked her about Seth, but irritated with herself for sleeping with her husband's son. What was she thinking? She prayed that Seth would never say anything to his father about their one night fling.

"No, I haven't and I hope I don't."

"Are you going to tell him that you aren't pregnant?"

"No, why should I? We've never discussed it and like I told you and Avery, it meant nothing. It was all hormones and nothing else. I don't owe him an explanation about anything. I'm just praying he keeps his mouth shut and doesn't tell Harper what happened. Something tells me that he won't."

"Well, I don't have anything else scheduled for the remainder of the day. If you want to go house hunting, I'll go with you. That is, if you want some company."

"Yeah, that would be great. I'll come by your house and get you."

"Okay."

"I'm going to get dressed. I should be there in the next hour. Will you be home by then?"

"Sure. I'm on my way there now. See you in a little bit."

"Okay, bye for now," said Eva.

Before getting dressed, Eva spontaneously called Harper. She was surprised that he answered. He was always wrapped up with hospital stuff. She understood him being the chief cardiologist and medical director at Adverse General Hospital, but dang, didn't he ever have time for family? That was what drove her to the arms of Seth. She wasn't trying to make excuses for her actions, but the truth was the truth.

"Hey, Eva. How can I help you? If it's more money you want, that credit card I gave you is more than enough for you to do what you need to do," he said harshly.

"We need to talk. I have something to tell you, Harper."

"I think you've told me everything there is to tell. You're pregnant and it's not my kid. What more do you have to explain?"

"We need to talk. I'll call you later this evening, say around six. Better yet, meet me here at the hotel around that time. You should be finished gallivanting around that hospital by then I'm sure."

"Goodbye, Eva. If I can get away, I'll see you at seven. If not, I'll see you when I see you," he said and abruptly hung up the phone.

Eva bit on her bottom lip, furious at the way Harper was treating her. She went to the huge hotel closet to decide what she would wear. She settled on a bright orange romper with a pair of flat slip on shoes and a cute hat to set off her attire. She pulled her long, black hair up in a ball on top of her head, put on a pair of large hoop earrings with a coordinating necklace and set out to go meet up with Peyton.

"Be good," she said to her pooches before leaving the luxury two-bedroom suite with ocean views. A wood spiral staircase was in the middle of the room leading to a private terrace with more spectacular views.

Chapter 9

"Don't let anyone ever make you feel like you don't deserve what you want." Heath Ledger

"I liked that five bedroom house with the two fireplaces and the inside pool," Peyton said.

"I liked that one too, only what use will I get out of fireplaces in Florida? How many times do you know of that it gets cold enough for a fireplace? I like the four bedroom, four bath house. It was forty-seven hundred square feet, had a pool in the back yard, a beautiful ocean view, and the white kitchen with the huge island that I want. And I think it would be in the price range that Harper wouldn't put up much of a fuss about."

"You're going to lease it, right?" Peyton asked.

"Yes, why?"

"Because you act like it's completely over between you and Harper. You don't know what the future will hold now that you aren't pregnant. He might want you to come back."

"Do you honestly think I would go back to him just like that? That would make me the biggest fool," Eva said as the women drove to the next location to meet up with the realtor.

"Not necessarily. I do believe Harper loves you, but think about how he feels. It had to be shocking to learn that you were pregnant and knowing that the baby couldn't possibly be his. He felt the ultimate betrayal, I'm sure," Peyton explained.

"The ultimate betrayal was him not telling me he had a vasectomy. He knew I wanted children. I told him that before we got married. He should have told me and I could have made the decision to marry him or not to marry him, but at least I would have known the truth."

"I understand you too, but I'm still saying, the fact remains that you slept with someone else. It doesn't matter that it was Seth. What matters is that you cheated and that had to hurt him. It had to hurt him bad."

"And it hurt me just as bad because he was living a lie. I wonder when he was going to tell me the truth or was he going to keep stringing me along, telling me that we would have a baby the next year. What was going to happen when next year rolled around? Was he going to put it off again and again and again?" Eva threw one hand up from the steering wheel in frustration. "Don't make him out to be the victim, Peyton."

"I'm not. I'm just trying to get you to look at both sides. Anyway, let's get back to my question. What if he asks you to come back home once he finds out you're not pregnant. Are you going to even consider it? You know you still love the man."

Eva continued driving without responding. Finally, she said, "I can't answer that. I love Harper, but I don't want to be anybody's fool either."

They arrived at the next house. "This one has the best appeal of the two other ones. It sits back off the street just like I want. And I love this light colored brick and the columns gracing the front entrance."

"Yeah, and the long drive leading up to the house is cool," remarked Peyton.

"Check out the wraparound porch. And I can already see the ocean and we haven't even gotten inside the house," Eva remarked with excitement.

She parked the car in front of the four car garage and she and Peyton proceeded to get out of the car and walk up the steps and onto the porch.

"I love this," Eva said.

"I do too. I can see all the girls sitting out here sipping on iced tea and fresh lemonade. This is awesome," Peyton said.

Eva used the heavy steel knocker to knock on the massive double door. Shortly, thereafter, the realtor opened the door and welcomed them inside.

Immediately they walked into a large foyer that opened up to an even larger living room to the right and another gigantic room with hardwood flooring to the left. As they continued to walk into the house, Eva oohed and aahed over the luxurious crown moldings throughout along with a staircase that was elegant enough to welcome royalty. The house was over eight thousand square feet with seven bedrooms, eight and a half bathrooms, a family room, a white gourmet kitchen that was to die for, and a master suite that Eva could see herself never coming out of. She would be able to have her parents and her brother to come from Bolivia. Perhaps even move in with her, if her father agreed. The view in the back of the house was perfect. There was an ocean view second to none. She could practically walk out of her back door and be at the ocean.

"I love it. I love it more than all the other houses we've seen," Eva said to the realtor and to Peyton. "The only thing is it might be too large for me. I mean it's just me and my three dogs. And Harper will probably balk at paying the lease on a house this expensive," she said.

"Then he should have thought about that before he threw you out," Peyton whispered so the realtor wouldn't hear.

"I suppose you're right," Eva agreed, laughing in her hand.

"Let me think about things and I'll get back to you later this week," Eva told the realtor.

"That will be just fine. These properties go fast, so as soon as you make a decision, please give me a call."

"Okay, I will. And I might want to see a couple more before I make a final decision. Particularly, homes that are a little smaller, like under five thousand square feet."

"Sure, I'll see what I can pull up."

"And thank you for agreeing to show me houses on such short notice. I appreciate it," she said in her pronounced and heavy Bolivian accent.

Chapter 10

"Never let a problem to be solved become more important than a person to be loved." Barbara Johnson

Eva returned to the hotel to get her fur babies prepared for the hotel's dog walker to come and take them on their afternoon stroll. After putting on their leashes, she decided she would take them on their walk herself. She got out of her clothes and changed into a pair of short shorts, a t-shirt and some sneakers. Stopping in the fully equipped subzero kitchen, she removed an ice cold bottle of Essential water from the double wide stainless steel fridge, then remembered she would definitely want to listen to her music, so she went into the den area of the hotel suite, got her earbuds, and put on her fanny pack. She put the phone on a clip on her side and out the door she and went with the dogs tugging on their leashes.

Downstairs, she stopped at the concierge desk and informed him of her decision and asked him to cancel her afternoon dog walking service. Eva headed out the hotel door and began the walk around the area. The afternoon remained gorgeous. Summer was in full effect but the sun's rays were gentle as they bounced off her olive toned skin.

Walking through this part of Adverse City was heavenly. There were signature shops lining the street. The sound of life was prevalent. She walked the dogs for half a block before she turned the corner to the left, and walked another half block.

"Hold on, we're almost there," she commanded. A few additional steps and she arrived at the entrance of the twenty acre park where dogs were free to roam. She didn't remove their leashes, however, always afraid that bigger dogs would bully them. Most of the time, she laughed to herself, at the thought. It was her dogs who did all of the barking and bullying. Inside they must have seen themselves just as tough and intimidating as the larger dogs. She walked them around the park and breathed in the aroma of the summer day.

As they walked and each one did their business, she walked to a nearby stand, retrieved a scoop-the-poop bag from the stand, and proceeded to clean up after the dogs and place their waste inside the available disposal.

Walking through the park, Eva said hello to several people who walked pass her or toward her. Everyone was nice and cordial. She loved being in America.

As she continued walking, she thought about Harper and how he would react when she told him that she wasn't pregnant. In less than three hours, when she saw him, she would have her answer. She listened to some of her favorite Bolivian tunes, oblivious to the world around her. Clad in her comfortable short shorts, she took off in a light jog as the sound of the upbeat music filled her ears. Without prompting, the dogs began barking ferociously. Eva saw a dog almost her height approaching. It appeared to be a Weimeraner, usually a gentle dog, but her dogs could aggravate the most gentle of dogs...and humans. They jumped up and down, tugged against their leashes, and Eva almost fell to the ground when one of her legs became entangled in one of the leashes.

The owner of the Scooby-Doo sized dog rushed to her aid. "Are you okay?" He gently took hold of her elbow to help her steady herself.

"Yes, I'm good. Thanks. Hush, stop it," she chastised the pooches. They stopped barking but all three of them growled low under their breath, as if daring the Weimeraner to take one more step toward them and he would be annihilated. Eva laughed as the Weimeraner wasn't paying them the least bit of attention.

"Are you sure you're all right?" he asked.

"Yes, I'm good." She walked over to a nearby bench and took a seat. "Sit," she commanded her dogs, and they reluctantly complied.

The stranger followed and Eva found herself becoming a little perturbed. She had assured the guy that she was okay and thanked him, so why was he still in her space?

He extended his hand. "Quentin."

She gave him a weak handshake. "Nice to meet you, Quentin." For the first time since the brief encounter she noticed that he had a slight accent, like he may have been from the New England states or perhaps New York. She looked at him. He was definitely easy on the eyes. Coal black hair, flawless bronze complexion, teeth that revealed he had a doggone good orthodontist growing up and a body that said, 'I work out often.' The best way she would have described him to the girls would be that he was a dead ringer for the fine and sexy felon-turned-hot top model whose face was plastered all over the news.

"Mind if sit here?"

"This is a public park. You can sit where you choose. I'm about to be on my way. Thanks again for your chivalry. Have a good one," Eva told him, as she bounced up from the bench, and again got tangled in one of the dog's leashes. This time she went straight to her knees.

Quentin came to her rescue again. "You apparently are new to this," he said, flashing a smile and a grin as he took her by her hand and helped her to her feet.

In her native tongue, Eva released a string of expletives, directed at her dogs and at herself for being so clumsy. The dogs, including Scooby-Doo, looked at her with whimsical looks on their canine faces.

"Have a good one," Eva said, her face almost a cherry red from being embarrassed. She walked away, leaving the top model lookalike standing with Scooby-Doo and still smiling.

When she arrived back to her suite, she unleashed the dogs, and went to get ready for her meetup with Harper. She dismissed any thoughts of the guy whose name she couldn't remember. Unpinning her hair, her luscious mane cascaded down to the middle of her spine. She shook her head briefly, then began removing her clothes to take a shower.

The time passed quickly, and before she realized it, it was time for her to go downstairs to the dining area to meet Harper.

"I'll be back. Mommy's going to meet Daddy. Go get in your kennels," she ordered and immediately the dogs complied by rushing off to go inside their individual kennels.

Just as she opened the door to exit her hotel room, she bumped into Harper's chest. He was standing on the other side, his hand in a fist, prepared to knock on the door.

"Hi," Eva said as Harper helped to steady her. "I thought we agreed to meet downstairs."

"We did, but it was just as easy for me to come up here, so I did. If it's a problem, we can still go downstairs." Surprisingly, Harper sounded quite polite and laid back. His angry demeanor and tone was gone, at least for the moment, and it made Eva a little uneasy.

"No, come on in." *Why the sudden change?* she thought. She dismissed it, stepped aside and invited him into her suite. The dogs ran out of their kennels which was in the second bedroom and headed straight for Harper. They bounced around, ran in circles, and yelped incessantly while Harper patted and talked baby talk to them. He never particularly cared for animals, but more or less tolerated them. These three dogs had managed to soften his heart a bit with their love and affection towards him. He was glad he bought them for his wife.

"Can I get you something to drink?" Eva offered.

"Water will be good. Are you sure you don't want to go downstairs to the restaurant and get a bite to eat?" he asked.

"I *am* a little hungry, but I'll leave it entirely up to you or we could order room service. After all, they offer twenty-four hour en suite dining so, it really doesn't matter." Again, Eva was curious about the change in his personality. He had been so upset and angry with her ever since he threw her out. Whenever she talked to him, he was short, curt, and downright cruel at times. But this evening he had appeared at her door congenial, nice, and much like the Harper she fell in love with.

Don't over think, she said to herself, and went to the kitchen to get him a bottled water.

When she returned to the open area of the suite, Harper was standing in front of the picture window overlooking the city. He turned around as she walked into the room. He looked handsome as ever. Tall, rugged, and sexy. His brown eyes seemed to hypnotize her the more the space between them closed. Her heart beat rapidly, as it always did, when she was around her husband. She missed him terribly, but she was determined to remain strong and not give in to his sometimes demanding ways.

Harper accepted the bottle of water. "Thank you."

"You're welcome."

"So, what do you say we order in? I left the hospital, went to the house, took a shower, and changed clothes so I haven't had anything to eat since earlier today. And that was only a bag of chips and a veggie burger from the hospital cafeteria."

"Sure," Eva replied, "What do you have a taste for?" She had dined in the upscale restaurant on several occasions and the food, no matter what she ordered, was always delicious.

Harper told her what he wanted to eat. After she decided what she wanted, she called and submitted their requests.

While they waited on dinner to be delivered, they sat outside her suite on the balcony and watched the sunset. Few words were exchanged. The beauty before them seemed to transport both of them into a still, quiet, serene place.

A light tap on the door brought them out of their shared moment of tranquility. The dogs barked. "I'll get it," Harper offered and got up to answer the door.

"Thanks," she said.

"Quiet," he told the dogs. They trekked behind Harper in silence.

Eva took the opportunity to take out her phone and text Avery and Peyton telling them that Harper was there."

"Call if you need me," Avery texted back almost immediately

"Can't wait to hear what happened," Peyton texted. "Call no matter how late."

The server pushed the tray of food into the suite. "Where would you like to be served?" he asked.

"The balcony will be fine, thank you," Harper told him.

Eva was impressed. This was the Harper she loved and adored. The server set up the array of food delights on the balcony as requested.

"Anything else?" he asked politely.

"No, that will be all." Harper reached inside his jean pocket and pulled out a twenty and gave it to the server who in turned half bowed and smiled big.

"Thank you kindly, sir. Please let me know if there is anything else you need and I will gladly get it for you," he offered before turning and walking away. Harper walked with him to the door, closing it behind the pleasant gentleman.

Returning to the balcony, he told the dogs who were following his every move, "Go to your kennels," and they retreated.

Both of them ordered medium well steaks. Eva had a mixed salad and Harper a Cobb salad. He had grilled asparagus, cheese potatoes, and a small loaf of brown bread. Eva dined on her steak, steamed broccoli smothered in cheese, a loaf of brown bread, and steamed vegetables. Their server also brought two carafes of sweet tea with slices of lemon. For dessert she had ordered a chocolate cheesecake and Harper banana mousse.

Harper sat down in his chair at the balcony table. Reaching out toward Eva, he took hold of her dainty, manicured hand, and offered a prayer of thanks for their food.

"Can't wait to dig in," Harper said, and began to do just that, cutting into his tender steak and placing a forkful in his mouth. "Ummm, perfect," he said.

Eva did the same, and agreed with him that the food was excellent. As they dined, Harper finally addressed the elephant in the room.

"So what do you have that's so important that you needed to see me?" he asked, not once inquiring about the state of her health. That was something that slightly put her off because as far as he knew, she was pregnant, yet not once had he bothered to ask her how she was doing or feeling.

Eva continued to chew her food while poking around in her plate for the next perfect bite. She stopped, took a swallow of her tea that the server poured into both of their glasses before leaving, then looked at Harper nervously.

"I'm surprised at your pleasant attitude first of all. What gives with that?"

Harper looked up from his plate of food and at her. "I realize that I haven't been the nicest guy in the world. I tell my staff all the time that it doesn't cost anything to be nice and kind to others, yet here I was being exceptionally cruel to you."

Eva shifted her plucked eyebrows and slightly tilted her head while looking and listening to Harper.

"I'm surprised to hear you say that because even earlier today you didn't exactly sound thrilled when I told you that I wanted to talk to you in person."

Harper took his napkin and wiped his mouth then took a swallow of water. "You're exactly right. But right before leaving the hospital I had a patient to die. She was around your age. Had her whole life ahead of her. A husband, a little girl that had just turned a year old. I performed heart surgery earlier this week on her for a defect that she nor her family were aware that she had. I thought she would pull through. She seemed to be doing well, but then she took an unexpected turn and I couldn't save her life. "

"Harper, you've been a doctor since you were, well since you were what in your early thirties? You've seen patients in my country that you were unable to save."

Harper nodded.

"You've seen patients right here in the states that have died too. That's part of being a doctor, and part of being a surgeon too, especially a cardiologist. You can't save everybody. So I guess I don't understand why this patient's death has had such an effect on you. I know it can't be easy when a person dies on your watch, but I'm just saying you know it can happen and that it has happened."

"Yes, and you're right, and when it does it still hurts just as much as it hurt the first time I had a patient to die. The sadness you feel never diminishes."

This time, Eva reached over and placed her hand gently on top of Harper's and lightly massaged it with the tips of her fingers. It was her way of letting him know that she understood.

"Anyway, what is it that you wanted to tell me?"

Eva pulled her hand away. Clearing her throat, she said, "I went to see my gynecologist the other day so he could tell me exactly how far along I am."

Harper appeared uneasy as he shifted his weight in his chair. He nervously took several bites of his food, followed by a swallow of tea. "What does this have to do with me?"

"I took three at home pregnancy tests and they were all positive. I haven't had a period for the last two months other than some spotting."

"I don't want to listen to any more of this, Eva. I get it. You're pregnant with another man's kid. Why aren't you having this talk with him?"

Eva didn't address Harper. Instead she continued talking. "The doctor did an ultrasound scan on me. I have several cysts that he wants to surgically remove. It would be same day surgery, and he'll perform a biopsy on the cysts just to make sure they're not malignant."

"Which they probably aren't," said Harper. "Did you come to Adverse City General?"

"No, the doctor's office was located somewhere else, but I'll have the surgery procedure at Adverse City General. Anyway, as I was saying, the doctor did an ultrasound scan." Eva stopped and looked at Harper.

"What is it?" Harper asked, seeing the uneasiness in her eyes and hearing it in her voice. "Is your baby all right?"

"I'm not pregnant, Harper."

"You're not pregnant?" he sounded confused.

"No. I'm not pregnant," she restated as her eyes cast downward.

Harper looked at her then slowly spoke. "I don't know what to say, Eva. I'm...I'm sorry you lost your baby. I know it wasn't mine, but I also know how much you wanted a child. I'm really sorry."

"Harper, I didn't lose the baby." She paused momentarily before speaking up again. "I never *was* pregnant."

"What?"

"I said, I was never pregnant."

"What do you mean? Is this some kinda joke?"

"No. It's nothing like that. The doctor said the cysts are what probably caused me to have the false positive pregnancy results. But long story short, I'm not pregnant, so there." Eva turned away from Harper so he wouldn't see that she was fighting back her tears. She quickly stood up, tossed her cloth napkin on the table, and walked into the hotel suite.

Harper gave her a minute before he got up and went to find her. She wasn't in the living room or kitchen. He found her in her bedroom standing in front of the mirror coifing her hair. How strange was that, but he knew Eva confronted hurt in an entirely different manner from the typical person.

"Eva, I'm sorry," Harper told her in the most sincere tone he could muster.

She continued styling her hair. "That's it. That's what I had to tell you. So anyway, I think it's time you leave. I'll put your food in a container that you can take home with you. Oh, and you don't have to worry about bringing it back," she laughed nervously as she turned away from the mirror to walk past him.

Harper grabbed her by her arm. "Stop it, Eva. You don't have to hide your hurt from me. I know that was hard to hear. After everything you went through to get pregnant."

Eva looked at him with pain streaked eyes. "What do you mean by everything I went through to get pregnant?"

"I mean you knew how I felt about having kids. And you're a young woman, much younger than me. I wasn't at home much. And after thinking about everything, I realized how could I blame you for your infidelity. You were lonely and you were vulnerable. And when you did discover that you were pregnant, well when you thought you were pregnant, naturally you would say the baby was mine."

Eva's Bolivian temper slowly simmered inside. "The nerve of you, you self-righteous prick," she yelled. "You think that you're so perfect, but you're a long way from perfect, Harper. You're selfish and you're conceited. You think everything is about you. You don't care how I'm doing. Not once have you shown any real concern for me as your wife. You're standing here talking about my infidelity when you, you were the man of my dreams. I loved you, and yes, one time, one time, Harper," Eva ranted while raising one finger in his face, "I had a moment of weakness. I'm sorry. So sorry that I did that. But I never ever meant to deceive you. I honestly thought the child was yours, but you, you never planned to have a child with me. You married me knowing full well how badly I wanted a child. We talked about it. You promised me over and over that we would have a baby when all the time you knew that it would never happen. You deceived me. You're an evil, mean person, Harper Stenberg," Eva cried. "Why, why did you even marry me? Why, oh, God why." She was inconsolable now as tears rushed from her eyes and poured down her cheeks like a rainstorm.

Harper grabbed her and held her in his arms against her will.

Eva fought against him as hard as she could until she was able to get out of his grasp. "I want you out of here," she told him. "You can have the divorce papers drawn up. I don't want anything you have. I just want out of this," she screamed. "How could you ever say that you loved me? How?"

"Eva, you're right about me. I'm so sorry. Sweetheart, I was wrong. God forgive me for deceiving you. I planned on having the vasectomy reversed but then you came and told me that you were having a child, my child? All hell broke loose in my mind. I thought how could she do me this way. How could you of all people betray me, Eva? I'm just as hurt as you are. Believe me when I tell you that I didn't set out to trick you. I didn't set out to fall in love with you, Eva, but I did. You were so beautiful, so kind, and so sweet. And believe me, baby, I loved you then and I still love you. But we can make this work, Eva. Believe me, baby. You can come home and we can work this out. I forgive you, honey. I really do forgive you," Harper pleaded.

"You? Forgive me? You've got to be kidding me. Get out, Harper. Please, just go," she begged, still sobbing and ran off into the bathroom, locking the door behind her.

Chapter 11

"When an inner situation is not made conscious, it appears outside as fate." Carl Jung

The scheduled day for Carlton and Liam's DNA test had arrived. Carlton entered Peyton's attorney's office and was met by Derek and Liam. He looked around for Peyton but she wasn't there.

"What's up, man," Carlton said to Derek.

"Hello, Reverend Porter. Glad you could make it," Derek said with mild sarcasm.

"Hello, young man."

Liam in turn looked at Carlton like he was totally confused about the whole situation, which he probably was.

Carlton looked at Liam like he was seeing him for the first time, and now that he looked at the kid, really looked at him, he didn't see an iota of resemblance between himself and the teen. Not that it was a requirement for him to look like him, but Carlton just made an unspoken observation.

"Hello, sir," Liam said in a reserved and mannerable tone.

Carlton returned his focus on Derek. "Is your wife coming?" he asked.

"I don't think so. I spoke to her briefly this morning. She said everything was arranged and it shouldn't take more than a few minutes to have the test administered. Her attorney is bringing in a third party to administer the DNA tests just to assure that everything is carried out legally."

"I understand. I want to thank you and her for making this as discreet as possible. Going to juvenile court would have assured a media circus, something I don't want and frankly, something I don't want this young man to have to face."

Derek agreed with a nod and Liam kept his eyes glued to his phone.

"You all can make yourselves comfortable," the receptionist came out and said to them. "Everything will be ready in about ten minutes. Would you like something to drink while you wait?" she asked.

"Nothing for me," Derek stated then turned and looked at Liam. "What about you, Son?"

"No, Dad and thank you ma'am," the boy said politely.

Carlton showed his palm and shook his head, "Me neither, but thank you."

"You're welcome," she said and disappeared behind the closed door.

"Do you mind if I talk to Liam? It won't take but a minute," Carlton asked Derek.

"That's up to Liam."

"What do you say, Liam. Can we talk outside for a minute?"

Liam nodded and the both of them stood up and walked outside.

"Look, Liam, I don't know how much you know about everything that's going on, but."

"No disrespect, Reverend Porter, but you're not my father. The man in there," he pointed toward the glass front door, "is my dad. I don't care what some test says. All this stuff my mom, and you have put me through is so confusing," the wise teen confessed.

"I know, and I'm sorry that you're having to go through all of this. But I want you to know if the DNA says that you are my biological son, I'm going to be here for you. I'll take care of you and provide adequately for you the same way I do for my other sons. By the way, which means you'll have four younger brothers to deal with," Carlton said jokingly.

Liam smiled. "Yeah, I know. I already know them from church and school."

"And I also want you to know that I won't try to separate you or take you away from your parents. But I would love to have a relationship with you if it turns out that you're my kid."

Liam looked at Carlton. A sheepish, childlike look took over his face in place of the strong, standoffish demeanor he displayed when they initially came outside.

"I'm not here to cause you to be any more confused than you already are. I know it's already a lot for you to take in."

Liam remained quiet.

"Do you understand me, Liam?"

"Yes, I understand. Is that it?" the teen asked.

"Yes, that's it," Carlton replied and watched as the young man turned around and went back inside the attorney's office.

Carlton remained outside. He removed his phone from off its clip and texted Peyton. "You coming for the DNA test?"

Within a few seconds, Peyton responded. "No, decided it's best if I don't. Was about to text you. I just texted Derek to let him know I won't be there. Don't want to upset Liam. He's still not ready to see me," she said.

"Understood," Carlton replied.

Carlton went back inside the office and waited until the three of them were called to the back. The receptionist was right; it only took a few minutes for the DNA test to be administered, but the outcome of the test would result in a lifetime of changes for them all, but especially for Liam.

"We'll have the test results in two weeks," the tester explained in the presence of the attorney.

"Our office will contact you when they come in," the attorney said.

"Thanks," Derek said, standing and shaking the attorney's hand followed by Carlton repeating the same gesture.

As they walked outside to their respective cars, Derek passed the keys to Liam. "Son, you can go to the car if you'd like. Oh, and get on the driver's side. It's the perfect time to practice your driving if you want to get that license," Derek told him.

"For real? Thanks , Dad." Liam's face immediately brightened and he ran to the car.

"Just don't leave me. I'll be there in a minute," Derek said, laughing as he proudly watched the boy go to the car.

"Look, I just wanted to hang back and talk to you a minute. Not as my pastor but man to man."

"Certainly," said Carlton.

"That boy is my kid."

Carlton nodded in agreement.

"I've raised him, provided for him, loved him, watched out for him. You know what I mean?"

"I do," Carlton answered.

"So I guess what I'm saying is if this DNA says that he is your kid, then I hope things won't change for me and Liam. I don't want a bunch of mess. The kid has been through enough already. He has to learn how to forgive Peyton and he has to learn how to forgive his birth mother, even though she's forever gone. If you're his father, I know you're going to want a relationship with him. That's understandable."

"I'm glad to hear you say that. It's primarily the same thing I was telling Liam when we talked. I wanted him to know that I wasn't going to interfere with you and his relationship but that, by the same token, I'm going to want to be part of his life."

"Just as long as we got that straight. My focus is on that boy over there," Derek said, pointing toward his car where Derek was patiently waiting.

"Same here. You're a fine man, Derek," Carlton told him. "Liam is blessed to have you as his father."

"Thanks, man. Guess we'll know what's what soon."

"Until then, you be blessed," Carlton extended his hand and the two men shook hands then gave each other dap.

Chapter 12

"You may tell the greatest lies and wear a brilliant disguise, but you can't escape the eyes of the one who sees right through you." Tom Robbins

Meesha's pregnancy was going without issue but she had made up her mind that she was going to have her tubes tied after this child was born. She discussed it with Carlton and he agreed. Whether he had agreed or not, she had resolved within herself to go through with it. As of now, their marriage was basically back intact, but she still did not feel all the way comfortable about the future of their marriage. She didn't want to believe that she and Carlton would experience something again like they'd just gone through but if they did, having five children to raise as a single parent would be trying enough without the possibility of getting pregnant with a sixth. No way. So getting her tubes tied was just a precautionary measure she was willing to take and anyway, five kids was already a village, a village that didn't need expanding.

She loved her sons and she enjoyed being a mother, but unlike most mothers with a family the size of hers, Meesha had Yulisa, the nanny. She didn't have to handle the boys on her own. Yulisa was always available and at her beck and call. But all of that could quickly change if she and Carlton ever split.

Dismissing the thoughts about the future of her marriage, she turned her thoughts back to making sure the boys were dressed and ready.

"Boys, hurry up. We can't be late for this appointment," she told them. Malik, Marlon, Micah, CJ, to the car," she ordered.

"Carlton, don't forget your phone. You're about to walk out and leave it," she told him. "Look, it's over there on the edge of the sofa," she said, pointing in the family room.

"Thanks, babe." Carlton went into the family room and retrieved his phone. "I'm ready. Let's do this," he said.

They climbed into the family's Suburban, the vehicle they used when they went on family outings.

The boys were excited about going with their parents to find out the gender of the baby. With every pregnancy, learning the gender of the baby became a family event. Afterwards, they would go out to eat, which was the icing on the cake for the boys.

"Remember, boys, no matter if it's a boy or a girl, this new edition to our family will be a blessing from God," Meesha told them.

"I want a sister," CJ said.

"I want another brother," both Marlon and Micah said.

"I want to go out to eat," Malik said, gruffly.

Driving to the doctor's office, Carlton detached himself from the chatter going on inside the car. He concentrated instead on suppressing his shameful thoughts and haunting memories but it proved futile.

Meesha being pregnant with their fifth child gave him a sense of both excitement and dread. It reminded him of his betrayal with Avery. Then his mind went around and around with thoughts of Avery. If Meesha ever found out that he had cheated on her with Avery that would be the end of it all.

At one time, he thought maybe, just maybe he was done with his marriage and that he was ready to start over with Avery. Whatever could he have been thinking to arrive at that conclusion? Was it because sex with Avery was out of this world and she did things in the bedroom that Meesha wouldn't dare consider. Or maybe it was because his affair with Avery would wash away the other sins of his past that Carlton felt were far worse.

He was glad that he had confided in Kingston about the affair. Kingston had always been able to make him see the error of his ways and talk some sense into him.

Carlton suppressed the rumbling anger and disgust he felt. He had given in to his flesh time and time again and his flesh betrayed him every time. He told himself that he was evil, wicked, a hypocrite, a farce, a wolf in sheep's clothing – and he despised himself for being so weak and so….human.

His mind continued to remind him of his past failures, bad decisions, and unmentionable mistakes. One by one, over and over like a broken record, they played until he reached the one that he knew was the ultimate betrayal. Betrayal, not just toward his family, but toward the God he gladly served.

Carlton couldn't allow the past to ruin everything he had built and as long as Breyonna was living, breathing, and spitting venom about him it was a good chance that among everything else he'd gotten himself into that she would not stop until his life had gone to the ashes. She knew things he'd done in his past that were sure to ruin him.

Breyonna was the real reason he initially asked Meesha for a divorce. She had started blackmailing him way before she showed up in Adverse City to so called claim Liam as her son. Carlton had wired her money several times to keep her mouth shut and keep her away from him and his family, but as time passed, Breyonna pressed him for more money, in larger amounts, and more often. She threatened to tell Meesha, the media and his church about his penchant for drugs, their sordid, sick sex life, his fetish for pornography, and of course her secret about Liam.

When she showed up in Adverse City, Carlton almost lost it. He had to do something to stop her. When she went to Peyton, he knew that everything was coming to an end. His life as he knew it would be over and done. The last straw was when she showed up at Perfecting Your Faith and caused a ruckus. She had to be stopped somehow someway.

No one but God and the man who had been his best friend since they were three years old knew the weight of the decision he made and how it bared down on his soul like a concrete block.

Klay Gentry and Carlton grew up in the same neighborhood and attended the same daycare. As little boys at the daycare center, they clung to each other and took up for one another. Their friendship continued over the years and their bond of friendship grew tighter as they became young men and lasted to this day. Klay was like another brother to Carlton. Being that Klay had no brothers himself, he formed an attachment just as close with Carlton and his brothers.

Klay was a good guy from a dysfunctional family. He and Carlton hung out twenty-four seven. When he became a teenager, Klay practically lived with Carlton's family because he was always at their house.

As Klay grew older, the Godly influence of Carlton's family rubbed off on him and he seemed to escape the perils of his life at home. Klay's was the too often typical story in a sad way—alcoholic father, abused mother, neglected kids.

As a young man of seventeen at the time, Klay met Allison, a nice girl who attended the same church as Carlton and his family. Like always, Klay was right with them, going to church every chance he could.

Klay was the first in his family to graduate from high school. He went to trade school and became an electrician. When he turned twenty, Klay and Allison, the girl of his dreams got married.

The first two years everything was going good for the couple, until Klay got wind that Allison was cheating on him with the dude who lived next door to them.

Klay never said who clued him in on what she was doing, but needless to say, when he got the call that Allison and the guy were at dude's house, Klay left his job and sped toward home. He parked his truck a half block away and trotted to dude's house. Peeping inside the bedroom window, he saw Allison and the guy. Allison was doing things with their neighbor that he had a hard time getting her to do with him. He felt sickened to the point where his mind went to a deep, dark, horrid place of no return.

He raced to the front door and hammered on the man's door until the guy opened it. The man's eyes grew so big they looked like they were about to pop out of their sockets.

With brute force, Klay shoved the man back inside his house and commenced to pounding him while Allison appeared wrapped in a sheet, screaming and pleading for Klay to stop as the man's blood splattered everywhere. Her screams only intensified Klay's anger. He bound their mouths, tied both of them up, went to the guy's kitchen and retrieved a bottle of cooking oil. He spilled a stream of expletives as he poured the bottle of oil over their bodies. Next, he pulled out and flicked the lighter he had in his pocket and.....set them afire.

Klay was serving a sixty-year sentence for their murders. That had been eleven years ago since his conviction, and he had become a model inmate. He was able to use his electrician skills behind bars and was often sent on various assignments throughout the prisons and jails in Miami and Adverse City.

Carlton remained in Klay's life, visiting him as time permitted.

Klay felt like he owed Carlton his life. It was Carlton who hired the best attorney at the time to represent Klay. Even though he got a sixty year sentence, he was spared from a life sentence and the death penalty. Carlton was his best friend and the only one that still cared about him. He was the only visitor Klay ever received and the only person who kept his prison books padded with money.

Carlton paid a jail visit to Klay when he found out that Klay was working at the Adverse City jail on a big electrical project. It happened to be during the same time that Breyonna was sitting behind bars at the very same jail.

Days later, Breyonna was found dead in her jail cell. Coincidence? Perhaps or perhaps not.

Breyonna, Breyonna God have mercy on your revengeful soul.

Chapter 13

"When you don't talk, there's a lot of stuff that ends up not getting said." Catherine Murdock

Peyton called Meesha for the umpteenth time. This time, Meesha answered her phone.

"I don't know what to say. I was expecting to get your voicemail again."

"And I started to let your call go to my voicemail, but I realized that it was time we addressed the issues like mature women," Meesha said.

Peyton exhaled, glad to hear that Meesha was ready to hopefully get everything out in the open. Peyton had a lot to say to Meesha. In the end, after it was all said and done, she hoped they could revive their friendship.

"I thought we could meet for lunch," Peyton suggested nervously.

"I have a few errands to run. I'll be free around one. We can meet up at Zodiac Café."

"I'll see you at one," Peyton replied. "And, Meesha."

"What is it, Peyton?"

"Thanks."

"See you later," Meesha replied and ended the call.

Peyton called Derek before leaving the house to see how Liam reacted to seeing Carlton Porter as the man who could possibly be his father rather than the preacher he knew him as.

"He did fine," Derek assured her. "That son of mine is a boss, I'm telling you. Just like his dad," Derek said proudly.

"That's good. Now the waiting game begins," Peyton said.

"Yeah, but however it turns out, I'm good and so is Liam. He understands more than you give him credit for. Now what about you? You still have plans to enter rehab"

"I said that I would, and I am," she told him. "I haven't had a drink and I had Elsa to get rid of all the alcohol in the house, including the wine."

"What did she do with it?"

"I don't know and I don't care. I told her not to tell me. She could throw it away, give it to her family, friends, or whatever. As long as it's out of the house."

Derek felt a tender spot forming in his heart for his wife. Could Peyton be serious this time around? Only time would tell. He prayed that she would make a serious change in her life for the sake of herself, Liam...and their marriage.

"Would you like to have dinner with me later?" he offered.

Peyton couldn't believe what she heard. Derek had asked her to dinner? For real? Peyton smiled with joy on the inside. If she could stay away from the drinking, maybe she would be able to get her family to come back home.

"Dinner sounds fine," she answered, hoping her excitement wasn't too apparent.

"Okay, I'll call you back and let you know the exact time. I think this time around it should be just you and me. I don't want to pressure Liam into seeing you just yet."

"As much as I hate the fact that my own child doesn't want to be around me, I do understand. I'll see you this evening, okay?"

"Okay, good deal."

Peyton looked at her phone after she and Derek finished talking. It was time for her to get dressed and go meet Meesha for lunch. She decided to wear a pair of straight leg jeans with a pure white off the shoulder button down blouse and a fashionable new sun hat she'd found on one of her many shopping excursions. The heels she chose made the whole outfit pop. She walked out the door feeling confident and rather happy that her life just might be making a turn for the better. God knows she'd been praying enough.

She got in her cream Maybach S600, pushed the ignition button, opened the garage door with another push of a button, and off she went. Along the way, she would go over everything she would say to Meesha. By the time she left lunch she prayed that everything between them would be back to being as normal as possible.

Chapter 14

"Good judgment comes from experience, and experience comes from bad judgment." Rita Mae Brown

Today was Avery's free day. School was out for the next three weeks, so she didn't have to take the girls to school or pick them up. Because of that, they had gone to spend a few days with their paternal grandparents, something they enjoyed doing. Ryker didn't have to go to the office until later that afternoon, so it was a good time to tell him that she wanted out of their relationship. She remained in their bedroom while he was downstairs in his office.

She picked up her phone to call Carlton to see if they could meet up later that day but he beat her to it because her text chime sounded.

"can u talk?"

"Yeah," she texted back and right away her phone rang.

"Hey," she said as soon as she answered.

"We need to talk," Carlton immediately said, but not in the tempting sexual tone she had become accustomed to hearing.

"Uh, I agree," somewhat startled by his brashness. "I need to know what was up with you and that little charade the other night at the pizza place. I haven't seen or heard from you since I saw you, Meesha, and the boys playing the perfect family. You have a lot of explaining to do."

"Don't start with the ultimatums, Avery. Just meet me in an hour," he basically ordered.

"Uh, okay. What about we meet at that quaint restaurant on Adverse Boulevard. You know the one I'm talking about don't you? The Bistro."

"No, we need some privacy. I'll get a room at the Westin on the east side. I'll text you the room number. What I have to say isn't meant for any other ears to hear."

"Okay, see you in an hour." She ended the call and wondered what Carlton meant. First of all, he sounded like he was angry with her and if he was, she had no idea why he would be. If anyone had a right to be mad, it was her after overhearing what Meesha said. If Meesha was pregnant, then this would possibly put a dent in the plans she and Carlton had to be together. And what would that mean for her after she told him that she was pregnant with his child, too.

"Hey, what do you say we have a little lunch before I go to the office," Ryker proposed.

Avery jumped slightly when he first spoke, not aware that he'd come into the room. She swiftly turned around while at the same time saying, "Ryker, I al..." She stopped in mid-sentence when she saw Ryker approaching her in nothing but the attire he came into the world wearing – nothing.

"What are you—"

Again, her words were cut off. This time by his lips on top of hers. He began slowly undressing her while continuing to smother her with kisses. She was weak to him, always had been and though she planned to walk out on their relationship, today was not that day. Carlton would have to wait. Family first she thought as Ryker eased her down on the bed. Hunger and desire rose and flared in her like a wild animal. She missed this part of Ryker. He could always bring out the best or the worst in her, depending on how one looked at the situation.

When they were done with their mid-morning lovemaking session, Ryker led her to the shower and made love to her again.

"I love you," Ryker said hungrily. "Marry me. Please, say that you will. Don't deny me any longer," he pleaded as his hand moved magically over what seemed like every crevice of her naked body.

At that moment, she was torn between her love for Ryker and her desire to start anew with Carlton. Her only answer to his question was her own sounds of satisfaction as she molded her body against him, wanting more.

Carlton had been waiting on Avery for well over an hour. "Where are you, Avery?" he said aloud as he sat in the hotel room chair. He glanced at his phone again, and again he texted her. She hadn't answered any of his messages since they talked and that had been three hours ago. He couldn't wait much longer, but he also didn't want another day to pass without him breaking things off once and for all with her.

Meesha was back and she was pregnant with his child. There was no way he was going to leave her. God had surely intervened and saved his marriage and his family, and for that he was thankful. He got up from the chair and walked over to the window and back to the chair. His phone rang. "Hello,"

"Carlton, I'm meeting Peyton for lunch then I'm going to pick up the boys from day camp," she said.

"You're meeting Peyton?"

"Yes, I'm meeting Peyton. She's been calling me for the longest and I keep ignoring her. It's time I hear what she has to say. Maybe we can put everything behind us," Meesha told him.

Carlton smiled. Although she couldn't see how happy he was, he hoped she would hear it in his voice.

"Meesha, that's great news. I'm so proud of you, baby. It takes someone with strength and resilience to do what you're doing. First, you found it in your heart to forgive me and now you're going to give your friendship with Peyton another chance."

"I didn't say all of that, but I'm willing to give her the benefit of the doubt. When she called me earlier, my spirit was touched. I knew God was telling me to let him handle everything. If I allow him to handle it, then I know everything will work out."

"Amen and amen," Carlton said.

A knock on the door made him jump. "Okay, baby, I'll see you later. I have a meeting of my own, so I'll see you and the boys at the house around five."

"Okay. Talk to you later. Bye."

"Talk to you later," he said as another knock came on the hotel door.

Carlton ended the call and walked to the door. He looked through the peephole. He opened the door. "What took you so long? You're over two hours late. I was about to leave," he scolded.

"I had some personal business to take care of," Avery said, still reveling in the hot lovemaking session she'd had with Ryker.

"Well, I don't have much time now. I have to be back at the church in about an hour and seeing that we're on the other side of town, I need to leave here in the next fifteen minutes or so."

"You talk too much," Avery said, walking up on him and kissing him.

Carlton eased her back. "No time for that. This is serious. We need to talk."

Her face fell in disappointment and she flinched at the tone of his voice. "I hope this doesn't have to do with the other night. So what, Meesha's pregnant. That doesn't mean we have to change our plans to be together."

"You can't be serious," Carlton retorted. "This changes everything. Look, I care about you Avery. I really do, but I realize that God has given me a second chance. He's restoring what the locusts have stolen."

Avery stiffened as she felt a shudder of humiliation. "Stop all the holy moly talk and tell me what you're saying, Carlton."

"My family came back. Don't you see? I've been praying to God for clarity and direction, and he brought my family back. Not only that, he's giving me another child. Surely, you understand that I can't, I won't, leave my wife and family now. I love Meesha, Avery." He stepped up to her and placed a hand on each one of her shoulders.

"You understand, don't you, sweetheart? Now things can work out for you and Ryker. You've said that he wants to mend your relationship." He kissed her on her forehead. "What we had was good while it lasted, but it's over now, Avery. It's time for me and for you to pour everything into our families, into our spouses. God wants that for us. He's given us a way out of *this* adulterous affair." He looked around the hotel room as he emphasized the word this. "What we've been doing is wrong. You know it and I know it. Thank God, no one else knows about us. We can start fresh with our families."

"What about our child, Carlton?"

Carlton looked. "Our what?"

"Our child. I'm pregnant, too."

Carlton rubbed his head and began pacing nervously across the carpeted floor. "You're pregnant? Have you told Ryker?"

"Why would I tell Ryker when this is your child in my belly?"

Carlton shook his head. His expression was like someone who'd been struck in the face with a tire iron. "No, no, no, Avery. That is not my kid. Look, it's over. We're over. Go home to Ryker, Avery."

Avery felt like a fool. She'd been played. Shock quickly yielded to all out rage as she began screaming and curses fell from her mouth. She yanked the covers off the bed, swiped the lamp and TV off the dresser and everything else in her path. It was like she had suddenly turned into a human tornado.

Carlton lunged at her, tightening his strong arms around her upper body while she kicked and screamed.

"Stop it, Avery! Stop this foolishness." The more she kicked and screamed, the tighter he squeezed her. He put one hand over her mouth, almost covering her nose. She tried to bite him, but his forceful and big hand against her mouth was stronger than her own physical strength to open her mouth. He held her until she exhausted herself. When he finally released her, like a snake, she slithered to the floor, fell in a heap and began sobbing.

Carlton watched the weeping woman. He felt sorry for Avery and all that she'd been through, but what she was dealing with now, this was his fault. Everything that had happened in his marriage, his relationship with Peyton, Breyonna, Liam, and now Avery was all his fault. *Lord God forgive me*, he said in his spirit. Avery being pregnant could cause every brick to come tumbling down in his life, but so could the other ghastly secret that ate away at his soul day by day, bit by bit.

Carlton reached down and extended his hand to Avery. It was like all of her energy and strength was spent as she weakly succumbed to his offer to help.

She stood up and he held her in his arms. "Believe me when I tell you that I'm sorry, Avery. I never meant for things to turn out this way." He pushed her back and looked into her tear-filled eyes. "Listen, to me. You're a survivor. Remember when I told you that when I used to counsel you. You will get through this."

Avery looked back at him like she was in a daze. She said nothing, just watched Carlton.

"Everything happens for a reason. You know that. You hear me, Avery?"

Finally as tears continued to pour, Avery barely nodded in response to Carlton's words.

"I want you to cry all you want but when you walk through the doors of your home, I want your tears to be gone. Dry your eyes and walk bravely into your house, Avery. Then I want you to go to your husband like you're the happiest woman on planet earth. I want you to tell him that you're having his child, Avery." He lifted her chin up gently to make sure her eyes remained fixed on him. "Do it for me, Avery. Do it for the child you're carrying. This is not my baby, Avery. You know that, don't you? I'm having a baby with Meesha. You're having a baby with Ryker."

"This is Ryker's baby," Avery repeated in a comatose like voice.

Carlton used the back of his hand to wipe away her tears, then while holding her with one hand, he picked up her purse that she'd slung on the floor, straightened her thick, naturally curly hair which denoted her biracial heritage, and led her to the door. Before opening the door, he kissed her on the forehead one more time. "Now go home to your husband, Avery and tell him the good news."

Chapter 15

"Miscommunication is endless." JP Rattie

Meesha sat at the table and took in everything Peyton had told her. After taking the time to really listen to how the whole story with Liam, Carlton, Breyonna, and Peyton took place, Meesha believed everything Peyton explained.

She could only imagine if she had been in Peyton's place and she saw an abused and neglected child whose mother didn't want him or her. It broke Meesha's heart to hear what Liam had experienced as a child.

"Do you think he remembers being abused and neglected?" Meesha asked Peyton after they had spent almost an hour talking about the boy and how Peyton ended up with him.

"I don't think so. He wasn't even two years old then. But when I first took him to live with me, things were different. He had a hard time adjusting. He kept crying for his mother."

"After the way she mistreated him he still wanted his mother? Wow. Unbelievable."

"Keep in mind, she was all he had. No matter how badly she treated him, at the end of the day, she was his mother, so when he came to live with me, it was rather difficult. I didn't think he would ever stop crying and begging for her. Even though Breyonna had neglected him and someone, God knows who, maybe her, had beaten and abused him, he would still cry for hours for that woman. She had a sister but she wasn't any better, that is if she really existed because during the time back then I never saw any signs of her. Breyonna used to tell me that her sister took care of Liam, but when I popped up over to her apartment out of concern for her and Liam, no one was there with the little boy. The apartment was empty, trashed, and wreaked of human excrement."

"Oh, my God. That poor child."

Breyonna appeared while I was there, and that's when she told me her sister was supposed to be watching him. You know I told you that I knew Breyonna in college before all the drugs, and not once did I ever hear her mention having a sister. Come to think about it, I never heard her talk about her parents or anything. But the times I would see Liam, who by the way, she never called Liam. She always referred to him as that kid. Anyway, she didn't feed him, didn't keep him clean, nothing. She was too busy trying to find her next high."

"Well, speaking of her family, do you know who claimed her body?"

"The body stayed in the morgue for almost three weeks without anyone claiming her, so I did what I thought was the moral thing to do, and paid for a casket and grave site for her to be laid at rest."

Hearing how Peyton had intervened to save a little boy's life endeared Meesha to Peyton. She felt terribly bad that she hadn't taken time before now to hear what Peyton had been trying to tell her for the longest.

"I'm sorry that I prejudged you the way that I did," Meesha told Peyton. "Me, of all people. I'm always preaching about forgiveness and treating people fairly, and look at how I treated you and falsely accused you."

"It's okay, Meesha. We're all human. You didn't know. I feel like it's my fault for not sitting down to tell you the whole story."

"How could you tell me when I wouldn't listen? I was too busy thinking that you were messing around with my husband. I'm so embarrassed."

"Girl, please. There is no need to be embarrassed. I'm sure if I had been in your shoes, I would have felt the same way."

Meesha paused, took a bite of her vegetable curry with tofu, before she continued talking.

"And I never should have blamed you. I mean, Carlton should have confided in me. He could have easily told me about his suspicions about Liam being his son. He could have told me the whole story but he wanted to protect himself."

"I guess because that wasn't an easy thing to admit, Meesha. Carlton was doing drugs and wilding out back then."

"Yes, and that's still hard for me to accept. To know that my husband, a man of God was sleeping with another woman and doing drugs with her is something I'm still dealing with, Peyton. To be honest, it hurts so badly. After we sat down and he told me the story about him and Breyonna and the drugs, I'm telling you, I started to take the boys and head back to California."

"You and Carlton are meant to be together. I don't know why he was talking about wanting a divorce in the first place. Sometimes men can be so stupid, but then again, I try to see things from his perspective. Carlton would never want to tarnish your name or your reputation, and you should know that Meesha." Peyton semi-scolded her.

"Yes, I do know that, but it was hard to accept. I love that man. You and the rest of the housewives know how devastated I was when he told me he wanted to end our marriage. And then he wouldn't tell me why either? It was crazy."

"Tell me about it," Peyton remarked. "But all that's in the past. And you have another baby inside of you, his seed. Girl, you can't go anywhere."

Meesha laughed. "You're right about that," she said and rubbed her growing belly.

"I'm happy for you and Carlton. I'm glad things are getting back on the right track. I know it's not easy to forget what he did, but being the strong woman of God that you are, I'm confident that in time, you will."

"I pray that I will too, Peyton. Now, tell me about the DNA test. Carlton said the results take a couple of weeks."

"Yes, so I expect to hear something by the end of next week. I know Carlton is ready to learn the truth once and for all, and so am I."

"I think we all are. How are Derek and Liam? Do you think they'll be coming back home anytime soon?" Meesha asked with concern.

"I hope so. Please pray that they will. I need Liam to forgive me. Right now, he's so angry with me, and to be honest, I don't know why."

"Yes, you do."

"What do you mean?" Peyton asked.

"You said it earlier. No matter how bad of a mother Breyonna was to Liam, she's his mother. He probably feels that you deprived him of knowing her, being around her, having a relationship with her."

"I admit that I did, but you heard the way my child was living."

"But he doesn't remember that. I can believe that now because if he did, then he would understand as he grew up that you were the best thing that ever happened to him. God put you in the right place at the right time. And God knows Carlton wasn't acting responsibly because as soon as that woman told him she had a child with him, he should have been trying to get that little boy."

"Talk is cheap and you have to remember that Breyonna was a dope fiend, Meesha. Carlton never saw a child, never even saw Breyonna when she was pregnant. I honestly believe he thought she was lying, and I would have too."

"Yeah, you're right. See, you did it again," Meesha said.

"Did what again?" Peyton asked, taking a swallow of her Perignon water.

"You made me see things like they really are. I'm praying that your family will be restored and that both Derek and Liam will find it in their hearts to forgive you, and that they will come back home where they belong."

"I'm going to check myself into rehab as soon as the DNA test results come back."

"Oh my, God. You are? Oh, Peyton, I'm so proud of you." Meesha got up from her chair and went over to Peyton's side of the table and hugged her.

"Thank you, Meesha."

"God is so good. He answers prayers." Meesha returned to her side of the table and sat back down.

"If I want my family back, I realize that I have to do some changing. I refused to admit for years that my drinking was out of control. Derek tried to tell me. Liam tried to tell me. You and the rest of the housewives tried to tell me, but I wouldn't listen. But losing my family stirred something in me. I mean they didn't leave until all of this stuff hit the news media about Breyonna, Carlton and me, but it was the catalyst that led to the uncovering of my drinking problem. I told Elsa to get rid of every trace of alcohol floating around in that house."

"Now that's a serious move right there," Meesha said and smiled. "I'm not laughing at you, by any means, but I am smiling because I can't believe what I missed while I was gone."

This time Peyton smiled. "I told Derek my plans."

"What did he say?"

"Not much. I don't think he believes me, and I don't blame him. How many times have I said I'm going to cut back on drinking or that I'm going to stop altogether, only to go right back to getting wasted."

"You can do it, Peyton. I know that you can."

"Well, at least he asked me out to dinner. Do you think that could be the start of us possibly getting back together?"

"Whaaat? Are you kidding me. Of course. I believe it's a real good start. Dinner? Oh yeah. You know you got to be looking good."

The ladies broke out in laughter.

"Real good," Peyton added and they continued to laugh.

"Let's hurry up and finish eating so we can go get you something special to wear for this dinner date."

"I'm not going to argue with you on that."

Chapter 16

*"Let yourself be drawn by the stronger pull
of that which you truly love." Rumi*

Peyton didn't fully understand why she was so nervous about having dinner with her husband, a man she'd been with for thirteen years, but she was. Looking in the mirror, she studied her size sixteen frame. Now that she had sworn off liquor maybe she wouldn't have as hard a time losing the weight as she had in the past. But tonight wasn't the night to worry about that. Tonight she just wanted to have a fun night out with her husband.

Peyton was pleased with the way things turned out between her and Meesha. They were back in a good space and Peyton hoped that they could remain good friends like they always were. One thing she didn't want to tell Meesha and she didn't, was that she didn't think Carlton had asked for a divorce on account of Breyonna. Peyton believed something far deeper had been going on in Carlton's life, and no one, at least none of the housewives knew what that was. But like her daddy used to say, secrets don't stay hidden forever, they're going to eventually come to the light. Peyton hoped that Meesha wasn't around when the walls of deceit came tumbling down for Carlton.

The doorbell rang, followed by a knock, and then the door swung opened as Derek used his key to let himself in. He arrived promptly at eight o'clock, just like he said. He walked inside their home as Peyton approached the door.

"You look nice," he told her.

"And so do you," she replied. She thought he looked quite handsome in a pair of jeans with a solid blue shirt and a pair of black dress shoes. Peyton was dressed casually as well, with a new pair of jeans she'd purchased earlier after she and Meesha were done with lunch.

"I thought we'd go someplace where we could laugh, talk, have fun all while enjoying some good food," Derek told his wife.

"Who do you think you're fooling?" Peyton asked, placing one hand on her hip and laughing. "Come on, I'm ready."

"What are you talking about?" he asked and turned around to head back out the front door. He waited until Peyton had stepped all the way outside before he locked the door. "Peyton, did you hear me. What are you talking about?" he asked again, still chuckling.

"What other place in the whole United States of America do you love to go to? When we go to Beverly Hills, you go there. When we go to Las Vegas, you go there, and I'm certain that if we ever go back to Singapore that you won't leave that country until you've gone there. So cut it out."

"Woman, what in the world are you talking about?" Derek continued to jokingly pressure Peyton.

"Let's go eat. I only had a chef salad today and I'm hungry. So where is this place where we can laugh, talk, have fun all while enjoying some good food? Wherever could it be?" Peyton asked jokingly as they got in Derek's car.

"We haven't eaten at Y…"

"I knew it," Peyton quipped.

"Knew what?"

"Come on, say it."

"I was about to say that we haven't eaten at Yum's Seafood in a while,"

"You are such a liar. You know darn well the only place you want to go eat that begins with a Y is Yardbird Southern Table."

"Ohhhh, so you want to go to Yardbird tonight, huh." Derek laughed even harder than before. "That suits me just fine, ma lady."

They exchanged light conversation on the drive to Miami where Yardbird was located. It had been some time since Peyton had gone out just for pure fun's sake. She and Derek and some of their friends would sometimes meet up on the weekends to hang, but that stopped a few years ago. She didn't know why, only that they no longer did.

The conversation shifted to Liam. "How's our son?"

"He's good. I think he's about ready for us to come back home."

Peyton's eyebrows lifted, happy to hear that her only child was ready to come home. Just hearing Derek say that gave her even more reason to get her life in order. No matter what the outcome of the DNA results, she was going to rehab the following week after the results came back.

"Oh, thank you, God. So when are you bringing him back?"

"I don't know about that. I said he wants to come home, but he's still upset with you, Peyton. The kid feels betrayed and lied to. You should understand that."

Peyton looked out the window as they drove along the scenic street lined with designer shops, fancy high priced cars passing, and people of all kinds walking up and down the busy street. Her countenance had changed in an instant from bright and happy to sad and disappointed.

"I'm trying, Derek, but I'm also trying to deal with and understand the reason you took him and left in the first place. It's not what families do. You don't just up and bale when a situation gets heated. You stay and try to work things out for the sake of keeping your family together."

They arrived at the restaurant and the parking lot was packed. Derek circled around the block several times but each time he whipped back around to the restaurant there was no available parking. After about ten minutes of riding around, he finally happened upon a car pulling out of a street space. He pulled in behind him and scooped the parking space. It meant they had to walk about a half block to get to the restaurant, but the evening was crispy clear, and the temperature was just right with enough of a breeze to keep them comfortable and not sweaty and hot.

"You haven't said anything about what I said," Peyton addressed Derek as they made the trek to the restaurant.

"Just thinking about it."

"What's there to think about? You don't agree? You've always believed in family. You love yours and you've always taken up for them whether right or wrong."

"Liam and I didn't leave you."

"How can you say that? You left me as soon as things got heated; as soon as things hit the fan with Breyonna."

Derek looked at his wife, paused, and then continued talking. "You've been drinking for years. You're an alcoholic, Peyton. You think that the Breyonna incident is what tore our family apart?"

"Of course, I know things weren't perfect in our marriage but you never moved out."

"The situation with you, Bishop Porter, and Breyonna was just it for me. You hear me?"

They walked up to the doors of the restaurant. Derek opened the door for Peyton to allow her and a couple of people behind them to enter.

He approached the hostess counter and gave them his name. She searched for the reservation. "It'll be just a few minutes," she told Derek politely.

"Thank you," Derek responded.

"I don't follow you," Peyton said, picking the conversation back up.

"Let's wait until we're seated to finish this," he said, speaking low and almost in her ear.

Peyton was quiet. She couldn't wait to be seated so she could hear Derek explain what she thought was absolute nonsense. Their marriage wasn't the greatest but it wasn't the worse either, so for him to take their son and leave her like she was the world's worse wife and mother was unwarranted.

"Hudson, party of two," the hostess called.

Derek and Peyton walked up to the hostess.

"Follow me please," she said.

She took them to their reserved seat. Almost as soon as they sat down, a server approached asking for their drink orders. Derek and Peyton gave their orders. After the server left, there was silence at the table.

Derek felt like the night was not going to be as fun and upbeat as he had anticipated. Leave it to Peyton to dampen the mood and ruin what should have been a relaxing, enjoyable time. He hoped that maybe this would be the start of them working on their marriage again, but he had immediately had a change of heart when Peyton refused to own up to her insatiable thirst for alcohol being the cause of their marital problems.

The server returned with their drinks and then requested their orders, which they gave her. Again, when the server retreated, the silence between them deepened until Peyton spoke up.

"I'm tired of being blamed for everything that's wrong in our marriage and family. You're not exactly Mr. Perfect you know."

Derek sighed deeply, looked around and then across the table at Peyton. "You know this is exactly what I'm talking about. We can never go anywhere or do anything without having to deal with bullcrap."

"Bullcrap?! Talking about the survival of our family is bullcrap?"

"You know darn well I'm not saying that. That's another thing; you're always twisting my words. You have a problem admitting certain things, namely your alcohol problem." Derek spoke with anger. He was becoming more and more fed up with the situation between him and his wife.

"And you don't give me credit for anything. You're talking about I don't admit this and I won't say this or yadda yadda yadda! Have you forgotten that I said I was going to rehab, that I was going to seek help for my drinking? Can't you encourage me and show your support for me at least making a start? I haven't had a drink in days now. What do you have to say about that?"

"So what makes this time so different, Peyton? How many times have you promised to quit throwing back vodka like its water only to get worse? How many times has your son seen you drunk as a skunk, or had to help you to your bed? How do you think that makes him feel? So yeah, it's not the matter about Breyonna and Carlton. It starts and ends with you!"

"I am not going to sit here and let you put everything on me."

The server brought their food and they immediately stopped their heated conversation. When she left they resumed the conversation at hand.

"You know what, Peyton. Do what you do. All I'm saying is don't sit up here and act like you're some helpless victim because you're not. And as for Liam, not once have you tried to talk to him about this whole situation. You've just resigned yourself to being the pitiful, poor, mommy whose husband moved out and took their son. Well, if you loved him so much you would be reaching out to the boy. He's not some toddler who can't understand or recognize what's going on. So what do you have to say about that? Huh. Have you tried calling him? Have you tried seeing him? Hell, no! You haven't cause Peyton is being treated so bad," Derek said, changing his voice to sound like he was whining.

Peyton reached over and slapped him with full force then immediately regretted her actions. "I'm sorry. I...I didn't mean to do that."

"I suddenly don't have an appetite. You can stay and I'll call Uber for you or I can take you home. What's it going to be?" Derek said, pushing back from the table and standing up.

Peyton did the same and proceeded walking off. Derek went to the counter and requested their ticket, paid for the meal, and stormed out of the restaurant. Another night ruined.

Chapter 17

"It isn't always a change of scenery that's needed to make life better. Sometimes it simply requires opening your eyes."
Richelle Goodrich

What started out to be a good night had ended terribly. But then again that was the story of Peyton's relationship with Derek. They never seemed to be able to get in a good place, not for long that is.

The drive home was done in total silence. When Derek pulled up to their house, Peyton opened the car door and slammed it shut without saying a word.

Derek pulled off before she could barely step away from the car. He was fed up with trying to make his marriage work. For him, tonight was the final wrap. For her to slap him, that was unacceptable. Had he done that to her, he would have been locked up and behind bars rather than back at the rental house with his son.

"How was dinner with Mom?" Liam asked when Derek walked into the house.

"It was all right. Everything straight?" he asked the teen as he headed to his room.

"Yes, sir."

"Good. Well, I think I'm going to get a little shut eye. Don't stay on that game all night."

"Okay." Liam paused then called his dad. "Dad?"

"Yeah, what's up?" Derek stopped and looked back over his shoulder at his son.

"If Bishop Porter is my biological father, what then?"

Derek walked back to where his son was standing and placed one hand on his shoulder. "It's not going to change what we have, if that's what you're asking. I adopted you when you were just a toddler. You know that and I'm glad you know that because now you're old enough to understand exactly what that means. I adopted you because I wanted you. I wanted you to be my son, and I wanted it to be done legally so that no one would ever be able to take you away from me. So you see, no matter what the DNA test says, I'm your father. I'm not saying Bishop Porter isn't a good man, because he is. And he's going to want to be part of your life, I'm sure. He told you that. It just means you'll have more people who love you."

"Thanks, Dad." Liam looked partially satisfied.

"Is there something else?" Derek asked, noticing the questioning look on his son's face.

"And Mom?"

"You know your mother loves you and misses you. She wants us to come back home."

"If that's the case then why haven't I heard from her? It's like she's totally forgotten that she has a son. I know now that I'm not her biological kid, but if what you say is true and she really does love me, then I don't understand why she doesn't want to talk to me."

"It's not that she doesn't want to talk to you, Liam. She just wants to give you time and space. Plus, she's working on becoming a better person so she can be a better mother. Look at what she's had to face for what she did when you were a baby. She risked everything to get you out of the environment you were in. Yes, she lied about a lot of things in order to do it, and she's paying the consequences now, but everything she did, she did out of her unconditional love for you. So I don't want you to ever question or doubt that she loves you. You understand?" Derek explained.

"Yeah, I do."

"Now, I'm going to shut it down for the evening."

"It's still way early, you know. You sure you don't want to take me to get a pizza."

Derek chuckled. "Take you to get a pizza? You can order a pizza. But what I think you're saying is that YOU want to go get a pizza while I sit on the passenger's side, huh?" Derek smiled.

"Uh, something like that," Liam agreed, and laughed.

"Okay, let's do this. I'm starving anyway," Derek said.

"You and Mom didn't eat?" Liam questioned.

"Let's just say, I didn't eat enough, and I always have room for pizza."

Ω

Peyton stormed inside the house furious and hurt over how the night had turned out. Derek blamed her for everything that was wrong in their marriage. He always managed to turn things around and make her the one at fault. Sure, she admitted that her love of alcohol contributed to their troubled marriage, but she wasn't the total blame. Couldn't he understand the secret she had to keep hidden about Liam all these years? It troubled her all the time and, yes, maybe she *had* turned to drinking as her vice. It helped her cope. Drinking helped her forget about her past. She was always the fat chubby kid, the butt of kids' jokes. She was the one pointed at, stared at, laughed at, when she was growing up and she still battled with her weight. But when she drank, all of her problems disappeared, albeit temporary. It was her coping mechanism. Liam had saved her life. Yes, she was a successful pharmaceutical salesperson back in the day, and good at what she did, but she was still troubled even back then. Until Liam. It was a blessing in disguise to hook back up with Breyonna because she received her blessing in the form of a little boy all because of the drug addicted Breyonna.

Peyton went to her bedroom and for a moment she stood inside the door and surveyed all of her manifold blessings. Beautiful, expensive home, top of the line ride. She walked into the bedroom and to her master closet or it could have been called 'master room' because it was just that large. "Look at this. Designer clothes, shoes, purses. The best of the best." She flipped through the rows and rows of clothes as she walked slowly through the massive space. She circled back and then walked back into the bedroom. "God, you've blessed me," she said out loud. "And you keep on blessing me even when I don't deserve it. But I'm tired of fighting against myself. I'm tired of hating myself. I want to love me but it's so hard. And if it's hard for me to love myself, how can I expect for Derek and Liam to love me," she cried. "I have all of this and yet I'm empty inside." Peyton walked over to her bed and sat on the edge of it and with her head hanging, she wept.

After crying until she felt like she was running on empty, she got up and went downstairs. The only thing that could soothe her was a good stiff drink of Vodka. "I promise God that this time will be my last, for real. I'll be going into rehab anyway so one drink won't hurt."

She walked to the bar and it hit her like a ton of bricks. Elsa had taken away all of the alcohol. Peyton rummaged through the cabinets, hoping that Elsa had overlooked at least one bottle of anything. Peyton didn't care what it was – wine, a beer, whatever. But there was nothing to be found. She opened the refrigerator. Nothing. She became somewhat in a panic as she began jerking open cabinets and pulling out pots and pans, searching for a bottle.

"There has to be something," she talked out loud.

She ran out of the kitchen bar area and went to Derek's man cave and looked in the bar there. Nothing.

"Dang, all I need is one drink. Come on, now." She was in a panicked state. She ran upstairs, grabbed her purse and keys. Running back down the stairs, she bolted out the front door like a mad woman on a mission. She drove to the liquor store several blocks away, the place that knew her because of her frequent visits.

Inside the store, with red and swollen eyes from crying, she purchased a pint of Ciroc. Dashing out of the store, like the drunk she was, she opened the bottle right there on the parking lot. With fresh tears pouring down her face, she took several deep swallows. "Ahhhh. Now things will be better. I'm going home and everything will be better in the morning."

After taking one more swallow of the liquid poison, then another, and another, she finished the pint of liquor. She pushed the ignition button, put the car in DRIVE, and sped off the parking lot.

Chapter 18

"Every relationship has its own problems. But sometimes what makes it perfect is if you still wanna be together, when things go the wrong way" Unknown

Eva watched as the two movers gathered the last of her belongings. Just as quickly as Harper had paid to have her things moved into the Setai Hotel, now he was paying to have them moved back to their home.

Avery, Peyton, and Meesha would call her a fool when they found out that she had moved back with her husband, and maybe she was. But they hadn't lived in her shoes. They hadn't walked her path. Harper rescued her from a life of poverty and lack. Harper made things better for her family. Every month he sent money to her parents so they would be able to have food to eat and clothes to wear.

When Harper came to Bolivia three years prior, she was working for literally pennies as a receptionist at the community center turned makeshift hospital. Harper was part of a missionary group called Matters of the Heart. They were a group made up of Christian doctors and heart surgeons that freely performed heart surgery on some of Bolivia's poorest. They fell in love. He married her and she came to live in the United States. Harper took good care of her, provided for her, gave her any and everything she wanted. Who was she to cheat on him with his son all because Harper wasn't at home at her every beck and call? It was who Harper was, a man of integrity, a man who cared about others. How selfish she realized she had been all because he wasn't in their bed every night.

As she watched the men pack her last remaining items, she looked around the luxurious fourteen hundred square foot suite. This hotel room alone would make ten homes in the area that she once lived in in Bolivia. If it wasn't for Harper, her parents and her siblings would be living in the same two room shanty. She owed him a lot and if it took the rest of her life, she was going to show him just how grateful she was. If she never had children, if Harper didn't have the vasectomy reversal, she told herself that she could still have a happy life without children.

Harper walked into the hotel suite. "You ready?"

She looked at him and smiled. He was the same Harper. Harper with the thick black eyebrows, broad shoulders, cinnamon toast complexion and the winning smile. She owed everything to this man. A man who she had betrayed by committing the most vile act of betrayal, yet he was willing to forgive her and take her back. The one prayer she begged God to answer was for Harper to never find out that it was Seth who she had shared her bed with.

"I'm ready," she said.

"Then let's go home," Harper told her, reaching out to take hold of her hand.

Ω

When she walked into the house, she stopped and stood inside the doorway. It felt good to be home. She walked slowly, as if she was in an unfamiliar place, looking around and taking in her surroundings. *There's no place like home.*

A familiar aroma filled the house. Eva looked up at Harper and smiled. From the aroma, she knew it was her favorite Bolivian meal, silpancho, a dish made up of rice, golden potatoes, beef, fried eggs and topped with onion and tomato salsa.

"Marissa," Eva called out to their live-in housekeeper just as Harper disappeared and went back outside.

"Oh, señora, señora," Marissa exclaimed, appearing from around the corner. She moved as quickly as she could with Eva meeting her the rest of the way. "I'm so glad you're back home," the older Hispanic woman, who didn't speak English very well, greeted. A big smile covered her face as she spoke.

"And I'm glad to be home," Marissa," Eva responded, speaking in her and Marissa's native tongue, which they did often when it was just the two of them. The two women hugged each other tightly.

Harper smiled when he walked in and saw the women embracing. He sat the kennel down then opened it to release the dogs. They dashed off and started running through the house as soon as he lifted the latch and opened the kennel door.

"Looks like they missed home too," Eva laughed while talking and looking up at Harper. He met her laughter with a kiss.

After dining on the delicious meal Marissa prepared, Eva and Harper sat outside on the spacious outside lanai. This time spent with Harper reminded her of when they were first married.

"Let's go for a swim," he suggested after the sun had set and the stars filled the summer midnight sky.

"Okay, let me run upstairs and change. I'll be right back."

Harper stopped her as she got up. "You don't need a swimsuit."

Eva looked at him curiously. "But don't you want to go for a swim?"

"I do," he said, standing up and stripping down to absolutely nothing. Eva turned a shade darker, somewhat surprised and embarrassed at Harper's brazenness. "Take off your clothes" he spoke, in a sensuous, sexy, alluring voice. "I miss you. I miss all of you."

She slowly came out of her clothing as Harper watched with eager anticipation. When she was done, they walked hand and hand and stepped into the warm salt water of the custom infinity pool. The stone work around the pool along with the soothing water fountain gave the area an oasis feel. That was just the beginning of Eva's magical night.

The magic of Harper's hands, the sensual heat of his naked skin combined with the soothing water, drew her to a height of passion she'd never known before.

"I missed you," she told him, barely able to speak as his mouth smothered hers.

Chapter 19

"Secrets are festering parasites to a relationship, devouring their hosts from within, leaving behind an empty hollow husk of what once was." Mark W. Boyer

The following morning, Eva lay in her bed, recalling the night spent making love with Harper in her own bedroom. She turned over and rubbed the empty space where he had laid.

Before he left for the hospital, they had an encore performance and Eva felt the happiest she felt since before she thought she was pregnant. She sat up in the bed, suddenly feeling hungry.

"Umm," she said as she eased up and sat in the bed. "A hot cup of coffee, one of Marissa's bacon omelets, a bagel with strawberry jam, would make this morning absolutely perfect," she said.

She called Marissa on the intercom. "Buenos días, Marissa." She rattled off what she wanted Marissa to prepare. "Thank you, Marissa."

"Si. Bueno, Madam Eva," Marissa answered.

It was still early, but she texted the other housewives anyway to arrange a Ladies Day Out. She was excited and couldn't wait to tell them the latest about her and Harper reconciling. They would probably tell her that she was a fool, but she was ready for whatever they came to her with because she loved Harper and no one could change that.

Meesha responded but nothing was heard from Avery or Peyton. Avery was probably busy with the girls, and would call or text her back. If she didn't, Eva would try to reach her later. Peyton sometimes slept in late, so it was no surprise that she didn't respond right away.

While waiting on Marissa to bring her breakfast, Eva took a hot shower. By the time she got out of the shower, Marissa had brought her breakfast and sat it on the side of the bed on the end table.

Still wrapped in her bath towel, Eva walked over to the covered tray of food, removed the top, and popped a slice of bacon in her mouth. Without asking, she could count on Marissa to always put extra bacon on the side. She sat on the bed and began to devour the tray of food.

As time passed, and she'd finished breakfast, Eva got dressed and decided to do some reading, something she hadn't done in a while considering how things had transpired in her life up until now.

Next, she called her parents and talked to them. It had been a while since they last talked. She was glad she didn't have to lie to them anymore about her relationship with Harper. During their separation, she avoided contacting her parents and siblings. That was no longer necessary and that was something else that made her heart happy. She told her parents the same thing she told Harper about being pregnant. It was hard getting them to understand, as they had not heard of such a thing as a false pregnancy. But soon she got them to half way understand.

"Where's the lunch spot?" Meesha texted. "You all can come to my house. I can order something in or run out and pick something up for us."

"Are the boys going to be there?"

"Yes, but the nanny's here so they won't be in the way. We'll have our privacy."

"Okay, sounds good," Eva texted back. "Any word from Avery or Peyton?"

"No," Meesha replied.

"K. I'll try to call them again."

"Cool. 12 good?"

"12 is fine. See you then," Eva texted. "If I don't reach the other girls it'll just be you and me. That cool?"

"Yep. we need to catch up anyway." Meesha texted.

After sending the text to Eva, Meesha scrolled through her phone to scan the latest headlines taking place in Adverse City.

There was usually something that she ran across that would make her laugh or just the opposite, cause her to shake her head at some of the things people did. Fortunately, one of the perks of living in one of the richest zip codes in Florida, there was very little crime. As she scrolled through the news, what popped up on her feed almost took her breath away.

ADVERSE CITY – FLA. (WSVN) - Authorities are investigating after they said two Adverse City Police officers were struck by a suspected drunk driver going northbound in the southbound lane on Adverse Boulevard. The crash happened at approximately 12:45 a.m. The officers were struck head-on by a Maybach 360. Fortunately, everybody is in stable condition," said Adverse City Police officer, Grayson Karr. Police believe the driver, 39-year-old Peyton Hudson, wife of Adverse City Bank President, Derek Hudson, may have been driving under the influence. According to Adverse City Police, the officers, both employed with the department for less than two years were patrolling the area at the time of the crash. The crash remains under investigation.

"Carlton," she called out, her heart pounding beneath her rib cage. "Carlton. Are you here?" She bolted toward his office, hoping he hadn't left yet. He had told her that he had a meeting at the church at nine, but maybe, just maybe she would be able to catch him before he left.

CJ appeared. "Mom, Daddy's not here. He already left," her oldest informed her.

"Thank you, baby," she said, exasperated. She went to his office, eager to call and tell him about Peyton's accident. She pushed the Number 3 button on her phone and speed dialed him; it went to his voicemail. She tried again and the same thing happened. Next, she texted Eva and Avery to share the horrific news.

"Lord, take care of Peyton and all those involved in that accident," she prayed while she texted them.

Chapter 20

"No one heals himself by wounding another." St. Ambrose

Carlton parked in the hotel parking garage and waited on Avery to arrive. While he waited, he grew angrier as he opened his text messages and saw he had seventy-five messages—all from Avery! He was used to receiving a number of text messages when he wasn't at the church office, but the highest was less than one hundred and that was from a number of different people, not one mad woman. This was insane. Seventy-five messages in a few hours, and almost two hundred since he ended their brief relationship a few days ago. Things had changed quickly, basically overnight. He resulted to putting his phone on vibrate because she would call him repeatedly throughout the day, saying the same thing she said in the text messages, which was begging and pleading him not to end what they had together. Then she would flip from begging to threatening to tell Meesha about the two of them. Today was why he lied to Meesha and told her he had a meeting early this morning. He had to handle Avery once and for all.

It wasn't unusual for him to have early morning meetings, but he hated that he had to lie about this one. The way things were going he had no other choice. He demanded that Avery meet him at the hotel so he could try to talk some sense into her.

He glanced up from the phone, after deleting the last round of messages from her. He hoped he hadn't accidently deleted any important texts from his family, but with the outrageous number of texts Avery was sending, at this point he didn't really care. When he looked up and out into the parking garage, he watched as Avery creeped through the garage in her blue metallic Volvo S90. He called her phone.

"Carlton, sweetheart. I'm here," she said.

"I see you. Circle back around. Someone just pulled out of a parking space near me. I'll be standing where you can see me." He ended the call and got out of the car, waiting on his nightmare to appear.

Avery circled back around like Carlton told her until she saw the available parking space. Carlton was standing in the middle of the empty space. The expression on his face revealed his discontent.

He stepped to the side as she made the turn to enter the space. When she parked and exited the car, Carlton told her to follow him to his car. She did.

"What do you think you're doing?" he asked as soon as she sat down inside the car.

Avery looked at him strangely. "What are you talking about? I'm doing what any woman whose man treats her all of a sudden like she's a side chick."

Carlton inwardly scolded himself for ever getting involved with Avery. He thought she was someone he wanted to start a new life with, but boy had he been mistaken.

"Avery, you've called my phone over two hundred times since I told you things weren't going to work out between us. You've texted me almost a hundred times What is wrong with you?"

"I miss you," she said, cooing seductively but sounding like a mad woman to Carlton. "For a woman who's having your child, I can't understand why you're treating me this way."

"Listen, we've talked about this." He was trying to remain calm as best he could. He didn't want to take the chance of setting her off and making things worse than they already were. "The child you're carrying is not mine. It's your husband's child. Why can't you understand that? What we had was good while it lasted, but it's time that we both move on, sweetheart."

Avery began to cry. "You used me. You got me pregnant and now you want to push me to the side like I'm nothing."

Carlton realized that getting rid of Avery was going to be harder than he could ever have imagined. For the first time, he really began to see that she suffered from some emotional and perhaps mental issues. He didn't know how to handle the situation. He prayed in his spirit that he would be able to say the right words to make her go away.

"Look, you know better than that. I would never use you. It's just that you're carrying your husband's child now, and you need to give him a chance. Lexie, Heather, and that baby growing inside of you deserve to be with their father. They all deserve to have a stable family, not a broken home."

Avery began to shake her head from side to side and placed her hands over each one of her ears. "No. No. No. No. No, she repeated.

"Yes. Yes. Yes," Carlton countered, taking the hand closest to him and removing it from her ear. "Listen to me. Avery," he said louder. "Listen to me. The enemy wants to destroy our families. That's why he fooled us. He fooled me and he fooled you."

Avery removed the other hand from her ear and looked at Carlton. Tear streaks showed on her face, but she said nothing. She just continued to stare at him. "He took advantage of us. We were weak and he stepped in and made us cross the line with each other. Don't you see that, Avery?"

"The enemy?"

"Yes, Satan, Avery. He wants to kill, steal, and destroy us. You've heard me preach that. I know you have. We can't let him do that. We have to ask God to forgive us for what we did. Okay? We need to ask him to forgive us for committing adultery."

Avery's eyebrows rose in confusion. "But why should I ask him to forgive me for committing adultery when I'm not married."

"You *are* married, Avery. Remember, you're married to Ryker."

Avery started ranting all over again. "I'm not. Ryker won't marry me. All of these years and he never made me his wife. We've been living in sin, Bishop Porter. Oh, Pastor, will God ever forgive me for living in sin?"

Carlton looked at Avery with pity forming in his eyes. "You and Ryker aren't married?" This was like something playing out of a movie scene. Was she telling the truth? He didn't know if he could believe what she said or not.

"No, we're not married. We've lived together all these years. I've given him two babies, but he would never make me his wife."

"Why?"

"He always had one excuse after another. Then month after month passed and year after year. I was never good enough to be his wife. I've never been good enough for anyone."

"That's not true. You are good enough. You're more than good enough. There has to be a reason, Avery."

"So you're blaming me?"

Carlton could see her getting upset again, so he reached out and took hold of her hand. "No, I'm not blaming you. I'm saying that there has to be something he's battling with, Avery. There could be a hundred and one reasons why he hasn't married you. I don't know."

He watched her body and heard her exhale. She was calming down again.

"Lately he has asked me to marry him. But I can't."

"Why can't you, Avery."

"I can't because I love you, Carlton. We're getting married after you divorce Meesha."

"I'm not divorcing Meesha, Avery. I have to do what God wants me to do. And you do too. You have to marry Ryker. You have to tell him about the baby you're carrying. He deserves to know that you're having his child," he kept trying to convince her. "And you have to stop calling and texting me, Avery. We can't mess up what we have with our families. Do you understand me?"

"Of course, I do, silly," Avery said and started laughing. "Look, I don't want to hurt you, Carlton, but there's something I have to tell you."

"What is it, Avery?" he asked, playing along with her.

"I can't see you anymore. You see, I'm getting married. I'm marrying Ryker and we're having another baby. Please try to understand," she told Carlton as she reached out and cupped one side of his face.

"I…I understand," Carlton said, playing along with her.

"I'm sorry it has to be this way."

Avery jumped out of his car and took off to her car without looking back and without closing his door.

Carlton watched as she got inside her car, hurriedly backed out of the parking space, and sped off.

He inhaled deeply and released a long sigh. "God, let this be the end. Please, let that deranged woman stay away from me and my family. And, Father God, I promise that I will never betray my wife and family again. Just please let this be over."

Carlton waited a few extra minutes before leaving. Just as he pulled out of the parking space, his phone vibrated. He picked it up from the console. It was Meesha.

"Hello, sweetheart."

"Carlton, I don't know if you heard but Peyton was in a serious accident this morning involving two police officers. I've been trying to call you ever since you left."

"I told you I had an early meeting this morning. But is she okay? Are the officers all right?"

"From what I read, they're all in stable condition. Oh, Carlton, they say alcohol may have been involved."

"Good Lord," Carlton said grimly. "Look, try to calm down. I'm going to Adverse General. Hopefully, they'll let me see her. I'll call you as soon as I find out something."

"No, I'll meet you at the hospital."

"What about the boys? Who's going to watch them? Isn't Yulisa sick?"

"She woke up feeling much better. She said she thinks she had a case of food poisoning. She and some friends went out last night and she says she think she ate something that didn't agree with her. And I shouldn't be gone that long. I just want to see for myself that Peyton is all right."

Okay, I'm leaving my meeting now and headed to the hospital."

Meesha ended the call and immediately called Eva and Avery. Avery didn't answer the phone but Eva did.

"I'll see you at the hospital," she told Meesha.

"Okay. I don't know where Avery could be. She's not answering her phone."

"She's probably doing something with the girls and Ryker. I'll text her and tell her what happened, and let her know that you and me are going to be at the hospital," Eva said, sounding nervous. "Bye."

"Bye," Meesha replied and ended the call.

Chapter 21

"Almost all of our sorrows spring out of our relations with other people." Arthur Schopenhauer

She should have told him when she first found out that she was pregnant. She should have done exactly what Bishop Porter told her, but she didn't. She hoped it wasn't too late to save her family. After leaving Carlton, a confused and mentally distraught Avery, drove to Ryker's office.

"Did you mean it when you said you want us to get married?" she asked Ryker when she appeared at his law firm unannounced and after her encounter with Carlton. She caught him right before he was headed to court.

Her mind was going in a thousand and one directions. She thought she would have a new life with Carlton, but that wasn't going to happen.

Carlton convinced her that the devil was out to kill her, to steal everything away from her and she needed to make things right at home. She couldn't let that happen; she wouldn't let that happen. All of her life, she'd been used and abused, mistreated, and pushed to the side. Carlton was right; she had to fight the devil off. She couldn't let him have her family.

"What sparked the change of heart all of a sudden? For the past few weeks you keep denying me, so what's so different now?" Ryker asked, as he put some papers into his briefcase.

She placed her hand on her belly. "This."

Ryker placed the last file in the briefcase, closed it and looked at Avery. A stunned look came over his face when he heard her next words. "We're having another baby."

Ryker walked up to Avery and kissed her. "A baby? We're having another baby?" he said with a soft laugh. "Are you serious?"

Avery nodded and smiled back at him.

He whirled her around then planted her back on her feet. "Avery, will you marry me?" he asked again.

This time, Avery responded, "Yes, yes, yes," she said.

Ryker kissed her again and then remarked, "I've got to get out of here before I'm late for court. Think about the kind of wedding you want. We'll talk about it when I get home tonight."

"Okay," she answered and laughed.

Avery heard her text notifier chime as she exited Ryker's office. She had several missed messages from both Eva and Meesha. The latest message is the one she read, which was from Eva.

`"Peyton in serious car accident. We're at Adverse General."`

Acting perfectly normal, Avery hurried to her car and headed to the hospital.

Ω

Carlton arrived at Adverse General Hospital and parked in Clergy Parking. He hopped out of his black Bentley and dashed inside the Trauma Center entrance.

"Do you have a Peyton Hudson here?"

"Pastor Porter?"

Carlton turned at the sound of his name being called. It was Derek. He turned to look back at the nurse. "No need, ma'am. This is her husband. Thank you."

"You're welcome," the nurse replied.

"Brother Derek, I came as soon as I heard. How is Peyton?"

"Miraculously, she's going to be fine. Both ankles fractured, one is an open fracture, but thank God it's not life threatening. But she's facing DUI charges. Her blood alcohol was three times the limit."

"I'm sorry but I'm also thankful to hear that she's going to be okay physically. Have they let you see her?"

"Yeah, I saw her for a few minutes before they took her to surgery."

"And the police officers? Do you know how they're doing?" Carlton asked a visibly shaken Derek.

"I didn't get much information because I'm not the next of kin or anything, but as you can see, the waiting room is full of officers. One of them told me that the two police officers she collided with are going to be fine. Thank God for that as well."

"Yes, you're right. It could have been so much worse. We have to give God all the praise."

Derek nodded in agreement. "She had just promised that she was going into rehab after she got the DNA results for you and Liam."

"Speaking of that, I just got a call from the attorney's office on my way here. The results came in early. They're here. When I leave here, I'll soon know if I have another son," Carlton explained.

"I see. Well, I'm not leaving Peyton's side. I'll find out the results when I can."

"No worries. I'll let you know as soon as I learn the results. I've prayed about it and I just want God's will to be done. But like I told Liam, if he is my son, I want to be in his life. I don't want to come between what you and him have formed together. I know you adopted him and you've raised him as your own. I admire you for that, Derek. I really do."

Thank you, Pastor Porter."

"Is Liam here with you?"

"Yes, he went to the cafeteria to get a sandwich. We've been here practically all night."

"When did she have the accident?"

"Around one o'clock this morning. I got a call around three-thirty this morning. Scared the crap outta me. I woke Liam up, and had to tell him the news. Man, that kid has been through a lot."

"He's going to be fine. God has him covered. We just have to keep him surrounded in prayer. He has you in his life and you're a good father."

"He needs his mother in his life," Derek said sadly. "Why can't she seem to get herself together? If I'm tired of the empty promises, I know Liam is. I'm telling you, as my pastor,

I don't know if our marriage can survive. Not after this. I want her to be okay, but this may be it for us."

Carlton patted Derek on his shoulder. He understood where he was coming from but he didn't want to encourage the man to give up on his marriage.

"It's not the time or place to think about that, Brother Hudson. Just concentrate on making sure Liam is okay and stay by your wife's side until she gets through this.

Meesha and Eva both came rushing into the hospital.

"How is she?" each of them asked as they approached Carlton and Derek.

"I haven't seen her yet." Carlton replied.

"She's in surgery. They have to set the bones in her ankle. Both of them are broken. They're not life threatening, and that's what I'm grateful for," explained Derek.

"Thank you, God," said Meesha.

"I'm glad she's going to be okay. It's what she's going to have to deal with when she's released from the hospital that I'm concerned about," Eva added.

Both of the friends remained at the hospital so they could be there to support Derek. Hopefully, they would be allowed to see Peyton after she came out of surgery.

Eva received a text from Avery telling her that she was en route to the hospital and would be there shortly.

Without incident, Avery arrived, just as nervous and concerned as the other housewives about Peyton.

Eva and Meesha got up and hugged Avery when they saw her come into the waiting room area. "Hey, where have you been?" Meesha asked Avery.

"Girl, we've been texting and calling you all morning. I said the girls must have had something going on this morning," Eva remarked.

"Uh, yeah, they did. And after that I had to meet up with Ryker to take care of a couple of things. But I'm here now. How is Peyton?"

"She's in surgery. She fractured both of her ankles," Eva told her.

"But God is good and she's going to be okay," Meesha remarked.

Avery acted as normal as her friends. She showed no signs of being mentally shaken or out of sorts.

"So is everything okay between you and Ryker?" Meesha asked.

"Yes, of course. We're better than ever. Why do you ask?"

"You and I haven't had a chance to talk since I came back. I was hoping everything was going well for you. You deserve to be happy, Avery. I don't know if any of us have told you, but with what's happened to Peyton, it reminds me of how fragile life is. It's best to tell our loved ones how we feel as often as we can. So right here, in the middle of this waiting room full of people, I want to tell you that you are an amazing human being. I'm glad to call you my friend," Meesha said.

Avery looked at her like she was seeing Meesha with a brand new set of eyes. What was wrong with her? How could she even think of being the source of breaking up a marriage and a happy home? Something was wrong with her. It was as if a light bulb went off in her head.

"Thank you, Meesha. That was nice of you to say."

"They're not empty words, Avery. I don't want you to ever feel less than. I don't want you to ever doubt how important you are to so many people. Your girls adore you. And you're the best friend any of us could ever have."

Eva teared up. "She's right, Avery. You have been my best friend ever since I met you. There's nothing I feel that I can't tell you. You listen to me without judging me. I love you." Eva wrapped her arms around Avery again and embraced her. Meesha joined in and they all had a group hug.

As they separated, Derek came up and Liam walked up seconds later.

"Hi, Avery," Derek spoke

"Hi, how is Peyton?" Avery asked. "Is she out of surgery?"

"No, not yet. I got a call from the operating room a few minutes ago. They said the surgery is progressing well. They expect it to be another hour or so before they're done. One of the fractures is an open fracture so it takes more time to set."

"Liam, is there anything you need, honey?" Avery asked him.

"No ma'am. I'm good."

"He's tired. We've been here since I got the call at three-thirty this morning."

"Why don't I take you to my house? You can get some sleep, eat, or whatever," offered Meesha. The boys are at home too so I don't think you'll get too bored." She smiled at him.

"Thanks, but I'm good."

"If you change your mind, just let me know. It's really no problem. Okay?"

"Yes, ma'am."

"Have you guys eaten anything?"

"We had something from the cafeteria."

"Why don't I run out and get you something. I passed several restaurants on the way. It won't take long for me to go pick up something and bring it back," Eva suggested.

"Maybe later. You want something, son?"

"No. I'm good for now," Liam said.

"Son, excuse us for a minute. I need to talk to your mother's friends in private. I won't be long."

Liam walked back into the waiting room and took a seat in front of the big screen television. He pulled out his phone and did what teens do.

"What's going on?" Eva asked first.

"Yeah, is Peyton really going to be okay?" asked Avery.

"Yes, Peyton is going to heal. It's going to take some time of course, but as far as the charges against her, I'll have to talk to your husband about that," he said, looking at Avery.

"Ryker will be glad to help. But of course, you know that," she replied and smiled.

"Meesha, Pastor Porter was here before you and Eva arrived."

"Yes, I know. He called me when he left. He's gone to the attorney's office for the DNA results."

Avery appeared uneasy at the mention of Carlton, but she managed to hold it together.

"He is? The results are back already?" Eva asked.

"From what Peyton said, it would be at least another week before the results came back," Avery stated.

"Yes, that's right, but sometimes they come back sooner. I guess it depends on how many tests are in queue; I really don't know. I'm just glad that all of this will be over and done with today," Derek replied.

"Or just starting today," Meesha said rather reluctantly. She looked in the waiting room at Liam. He could very well be her stepson. Any moment now, she would know for sure.

Avery replayed everything that Carlton had said to her. At first, everything was jumbled up in her head, and she couldn't make sense of anything. The thought that she had texted and called him like she had was insane. Was she insane? If she wasn't then why had she behaved like a crazy woman? Maybe there really was something wrong with her. There were times when she felt like she couldn't control herself. It had been like that since she was a teen, at least that was when she first noticed that once she got angry and upset about something, she became uncontrollable. As she grew into an adult, she used to think that maybe she was bipolar, but she never gave it a serious thought. She settled on the conclusion that she had inherited her mother's mean streak and revengeful temperament. Her mother used to pitch a fit whenever things didn't go her way and she took a lot out on Avery when Avery was growing up. In today's society, her mother would probably be labeled as abusive.

"You okay?" Meesha asked.

"Huh? You talking to me?" Avery replied.

"Yes. You looked like you were standing there daydreaming."

"Ha, I was. I guess it's as good a time as any to tell you ladies my good news."

"Tell us, tell us," Eva said. "Then I'll tell you mine."

"You ladies keep talking. I'm going over here and sit with Liam. I'll let you know when I hear something. Okay."

"Okay, thanks, Derek. We'll be standing out here," Meesha told him.

"Now tell us."

"You go first," said Eva.

"Well.... Lexie and Heather are going to be big sisters. I'm pregnant!" She clapped her hands and smiled.

"That's wonderful," Eva managed to say with a forced smile. The thought of what the doctor told her gave her mixed emotions. She was happy, more than happy for Avery, but it looked like the possibility of her having children was over. She and Harper were back together and she would have to resign herself to having a childless marriage. Had she made a mistake by going back to him?

"Eva, you go next," urged Meesha, then I'll tell you mine."

"See, this is what happens when we miss Ladies Day Out. We have so much catching up to do," Avery laughed as the girls gave her high fives.

"No, you go next, Meesha. I guess you're going to tell us that you're pregnant, too," Eva joked.

"How did you know?" Meesha said, laughing.

"Hold up. Are you serious? You're pregnant?" Eva said.

"Yes. Number five will arrive in five months! Can you believe it?"

"I was wondering when you were going to share the news," Avery said feeling like she was about to zone out again. *Control yourself. Remain calm. It's going to be okay.*

"What's wrong?" Meesha asked, noticing the strange look on Avery's face

"Uh, nothing. Congratulations, again," she managed to say.

You already knew, Avery?" Eva remarked.

"Yes, by accident. I overheard Meesha when she told Pastor Porter the other night. We happened to be at the same restaurant with the kids."

"Oh, I see."

"Another one of our kids is going to be about the same age."

"Yes, isn't that just the bomb?" Meesha chuckled, then she immediately stopped when she saw Eva's face. She didn't want to be insensitive. Eva wanted a child so badly and to have the doctor tell her that she had never been pregnant, had affected her in a bad way.

"Eva, I didn't mean to disregard how you must be feeling. When you told me about the false positive test results, it blew my mind. I'm so sorry."

"No, it's all good. I'm happy for you and Avery."

Avery walked up to her friend and hugged her. "I should have waited to tell you my news I'm sorry. I agree with Meesha. I didn't mean to be insensitive to your feelings. God knows I know all too well how that can make a person feel."

"Didn't I tell you that it's okay. I promise, I'm good."

"So tell us your good news, Eva," Avery insisted.

"Me and—"

Harper appeared out of nowhere. "Hello, ladies. Hi, sweetheart," he said, leaning down and embracing Eva and kissing her lightly on the lips. "I heard about Peyton. I came down here to check on her and to see if Derek was down here. That's when I saw you standing over here. How long have you been here?" he asked.

"Not long. I was going to call and let you know about Peyton, and tell you that I was down here in the ER waiting room, but then..."

"No need to explain, sweetheart. I really hate this for Peyton and her family. I just heard she's being charged with a DUI and probably any other thing they can tack on to it."

"Do you think she's really okay though?"

"Two fractured ankles, and one is an open fracture. You know, the bad news is that some people never walk again after a fracture like that, and she has two, but the orthopedic doctors will know more once the surgery is done. I wouldn't repeat that to Derek and his son though. They've got enough to contend with already. Baby, have you eaten? I'm about to have lunch. You want to join me? Of course, I'm only going to the hospital cafeteria." He lovingly placed his arm around Eva's shoulder. "Whaddaya say?"

"I say, I'd love to."

"You ladies are invited to join us. Right, honey?" Harper said.

"Of course. We were supposed to have lunch today anyway."

"No, I'll pass," said Meesha looking confused.

"So will I," Avery added, not understanding the display of affection between Harper and Eva. "I don't want to be a third wheel."

"Nonsense," Harper spoke up. "I can't stay long anyway. I have a surgery consult in an hour. I was only coming down to check on Derek but seeing my babe was an unexpected perk. Come on, lunch is on me," Harper laughed. "You all can chat it up after I leave."

"In that case, okay," Avery reluctantly agreed.

"Well, you're not going to leave me all by myself."

"Then lunch it is," Harper said. "But before we go, I want to go say something to Derek. I'll be back in five minutes, then we'll head upstairs.

"When did this happen?" Avery whispered to Eva as Harper walked over to Derek and Liam and began talking.

"That was my good news. Harper and I are back together. He came to the hotel. We talked, and decided to give it another shot."

"But the way he treated you. Do you think you can trust him?" Meesha whispered.

"You went back to Carlton, obviously," Avery said in an unexpected biting tone.

"Excuse me?"

"You heard me. You took Pastor Porter back and look at everything he put you through, so why can't she forgive Harper? You're not the only one who gets to have a pass, you know."

"I didn't mean it like that. And Eva," Meesha said, and looked directly at her, "I'm sorry if that's the way I came off. If you're happy, then I'm happy. I just want you to be happy. And Avery, I don't know where the sudden attitude came from, but I am not one to pass judgment on anyone. You, of all people, should know that."

"Don't worry about it, Meesha. Anyway, there's so much more to the story that I haven't shared with any of you, which is another reason we need our Ladies Day Out. If only you knew what really happened, maybe you would see things differently. Harper is not the bad guy you think that he is."

Harper walked back up and planted himself next to his wife. "Okay, you ladies ready?"

"I know I am. I'm hungry. I didn't have any breakfast," Eva eagerly responded, wrapping her arm around her husband's waist as he towered above her.

Chapter 22

"Relationships based on obligation lack dignity." Wayne Dyer

"That was a pretty decent veggie burger for a hospital cafeteria," Meesha said, wiping her mouth and pushing her plate away from her.

"My chicken sandwich was actually good, too. The fries were a little too soft for me. I like 'em crispy, but the salad was fresh," Avery remarked.

"Yep, I agree. My food was good. You see I ate everything on my plate," Eva said, laughing.

"The way you cleaned your plate, they may not have to wash it," Avery joked.

"Ewww," Meesha and Eva said.

"Now that Harper's gone, can you tell us what you were talking about when you said if we knew the full story we wouldn't be so hard on him?" asked Avery.

"Yes, what did you mean by that?" Meesha asked.

Eva looked around. "Had to make sure Harper wasn't still lurking around. I wouldn't want him to hear me telling our business."

"Girl, please. You know our husbands know that we tell each other everything. If they don't know that, then they're not working with a full deck upstairs," Meesha commented while Avery remained quiet.

Eva inhaled, exhaled then slowly began to tell them the whole story about Harper, his vasectomy, her pregnancy and everything in between. When she was done, she wiped the tears from her eyes.

"It's allright, God is a forgiving God. All of us should know that," Meesha assured her. "And I hope that you and Harper's marriage will be renewed and restored beyond measure."

"So do I," Avery said. "The only thing that I don't like is the way he threw you out. So you cheated on him, and that's horrible, but how can he be so willing now to take you back. And yes, I know it's because you told him about the false positive test and all, but still just be careful. I don't know if I would trust him just yet."

"But I do trust him. If it wasn't for Harper, my family wouldn't be living better lives. I would still be in Bolivia, poor, often hungry, and with nothing going for myself."

"Yes, I understand you, but I hope that's not why you went back to him," Meesha piped in. "Yes, you have everything money can buy, but money can't buy true inside happiness and love for self, Eva. Now if you really love this man for who he is and not what he has done or can do for you, and your family, then I say what I said, earlier – congratulations on reconciling. But if you only went back to him because you don't think you or your family can make it without him, then you're giving him too much power."

"I don't want to talk about it anymore. I love Harper. I was wrong to sleep with another man. I'm just thankful that he still wanted me back, and I'm going to spend the rest of my life making sure he knows that I love him and that I appreciate him."

Without saying anything, unconsciously Avery's brow furrowed, as a look of dissatisfaction showed on her face. "You can be so…ughhhh," Avery huffed.

"What are you talking about?" Meesha frowned.

"Please, don't start you two."

"She's sounding like Peyton," Avery said. "We expect Peyton to be judgmental and smart mouthed, but now Miss Goody Two Shoes has started passing judgment on people."

"When did you hear me being judgmental?" Meesha snapped at Avery. "You know what? Something is wrong with you. Seriously."

"Don't you call me crazy!"

Meesha and Eva looked at Avery like she *was* crazy.

Meesha threw up her hand, waving Avery off. "Anyway, I hope you understand where I'm coming from, Eva. We all have gone through some trying stuff lately, but with God's help, it's my prayer that we come out on the other side better for it."

"I hope so," Eva said somberly. "I really do hope so."

Chapter 23

"You can't wait around for something to become good, it either is, or isn't." Toni Aleo

With emotions running in a hundred and one directions, Carlton exited the attorney's office, still reeling over the results of the DNA test. The first person he called was Meesha.

"Hey there," Meesha said.

"I just left the attorney's office. I learned the results of the test."

"And?" Meesha replied, placing her hand over the phone and saying, "This is Carlton I'll be right back," she whispered softly to Eva and Avery. She stood up from the table and walked out into the hospital corridor.

Removing her hand from the phone, she began talking to her husband again. "What did it say?"

"There is a ninety-nine point nine percent chance that someone else out there, only God knows who, is Liam's father, but it's certainly not me."

Meesha placed her right hand over her chest, closed her eyes, and exhaled. "Thank you, God."

"It's over, Meesha. It's such a relief. I just knew he was my son, but God said otherwise. The sad part about this whole thing is with Breyonna being dead, that young man will never know who his biological father is."

"Yes, but he has a good father in Derek, and he can move forward with his life. He's young, and he will get pass the hurt, and everything else that's been going on in his life. We have to continue to pray for him."

"Yeah. What are you doing? I thought maybe we could meet somewhere for lunch. You know, like have a celebration of sorts. How do you feel about that?"

"Well, I'm here at the hospital. Peyton should be coming down from surgery anytime now. I at least wanted to hang around until that's over. I was actually in the hospital cafeteria with Eva and Avery. Harper treated us to lunch. He was with us but he just left to go back to work before you called."

"Harper? How did that happen? I thought he and Eva were a done deal."

"That's a whole other story. We'll talk more about it when I see you later, but I can tell you this much—she moved back home."

"If they can work it out, then we aren't the ones to judge. I'm thankful you gave me another shot, so I'm happy for them if they want to do the same."

"Did you say that Avery's there too?"

"Yeah, she is. Why?"

"Uhh, nothing. My phone broke up. I wasn't sure what you said," he quickly lied.

"You know what, you're right about Eva and Harper. If they want to give things another go, who am I to say anything different."

"Since you're going to be at the hospital for a minute, I guess I'll stop and get a bite to eat. I'll probably call home to see if the boys have eaten lunch yet. If they haven't I'll take something home for them."

"I'm sure they'd like that."

"Yeah, so just call me when Peyton comes down from surgery. I'll come back to the hospital then."

"Okay."

"Talk to you later," Carlton said.

"And Carlton, congratulations."

"I'm just glad it's all over. When Peyton hears this, she'll probably be just as stunned as I was to know that I'm not Liam's father."

"Maybe she will and maybe she won't. All I know is that I'm glad you are not the father."

"You can say that again. Anyway, we'll talk later."

"Okay. Buh-bye."

To learn that Liam wasn't his kid was a huge relief. He honestly thought the boy was his son, but DNA doesn't lie so Carlton rejoiced. Then he thought about how he almost ruined everything by getting involved with Avery. Thank

God Avery had totally backed off. They hadn't had any real communication after he was finally able to convince her to believe that the baby inside of her was Ryker's and not his. He used his gift of gab to make the woman have a total change of heart, and he hoped that their affair was history. For a minute, he thought she was crazy as heck. But God had spared him from a situation that could only have messed up his life and his ministry. Now all he had to do was keep his nose clean and do the right thing by his family. Yet, part of him was curious about whose kid it really was that Avery was carrying.

Meesha returned to the cafeteria to share the news with Eva and Avery. As she walked back into the almost empty cafeteria she looked at Avery. What in the world was wrong with her? It wasn't like her to be so snappy and short.

"Guess we all have our days," Meesha said under her breath as she approached the table and sat back down.

"It's Derek," said Eva, reading her text message. "He says Peyton is out of surgery and in recovery. We'd better get back to the Waiting Room."

The three of them got up and walked out of the cafeteria and toward the elevator.

"How did the surgery go?" Eva asked as the three friends walked up to Derek and Liam who were standing outside of the Waiting Room.

"The doctor just came and talked to me. He said the surgery went well. She's going to have a long recovery, but he's hopeful that she'll walk again."

"Thank you, God," Meesha said.

"I'm so glad she's okay," Avery said.

"Liam, aren't you glad your mother is going to be okay?" Eva asked, walking up and giving him a side hug.

"Yes, ma'am."

"Have you talked to your husband?" Derek asked, looking at Meesha.

"Yes, I just talked to him. He told me everything," she replied without saying anything about the DNA results in front of Liam. She wasn't sure if Derek had told him about the results yet.

"Okay, good," Derek said. "It may be some time before Peyton will be up to visitors so if you ladies want to leave, I'll call or text you to let you know when she can receive visitors. I'm waiting on Ryker to call me back. I talked to him and he's working on addressing the DUI charges and any other added charges. He said he's going to meet with the judge about setting bond, get it paid, and that way when she's discharged from here, which probably won't be until tomorrow or the next day, she won't have to go through the humiliating process of being booked into jail."

"I hope he can work everything out," Eva said.

"He feels confident that he can."

"Don't worry; Ryker is good at what he does. Why do you think all the celebrities, ballers, and the wealthiest of the wealthy come to him," Avery spoke up.

"Exactly," Derek stated.

"Since you say we can't see her tonight, then I'm going to head home," Meesha said.

"I am too," followed Eva. "Derek, call me if you need me."

"Well, I'm right behind you. Liam, do you want to come home with me?" Avery asked.

"No, I'm going to stay here with my dad," the teen said.

"Okay, but if you change your mind, just have your dad to give me a call and I'll come back and pick you up."

"Yes, ma'am."

"See you all later," Avery said, walking off and through the exit doors.

"Do you want me to bring you something back to eat?" Meesha asked.

"Uhhh, okay," he said, looking at his father.

"It's okay with me," Derek confirmed.

"Fine, what do you want?"

"There's a Mexican restaurant and a Chinese restaurant on the next street," Derek suggested. "What about something from one of those places?"

"That'll be fine," Liam said nonchalantly.

"Here you go." Derek reached into his pocket, pulled out his wallet and took out a fifty dollar bill.

"No, I've got it," Meesha said, pushing the money back. "What do you want? Derek, do you want something too?"

"Yes, thanks."

Father and son decided on Chinese. Liam asked for plain fried rice and spring rolls and Derek asked for veggie lo mien and spring rolls.

"Why don't I take you over there. That way you won't have to go get your car and then park it again to bring the food back in," Eva offered.

"No, you don't have to do that, Eva," Derek insisted. "Meesha, just give me a call when you're outside, and me or Liam will come out and get the food," Derek told her.

"Okay, then I'll be back as soon as I can."

Eva hugged Derek and Liam. "Call me if you need me," she said. "Meesha, come on, I'll walk out with you."

24

"Sons are the anchors of a mother's life." Sophocles

Peyton had been wheelchair bound since being released from the hospital four weeks prior. The orthopedic surgeon had told her that she was to put no weight on her legs for at least eight weeks. After that time, she would be reevaluated and a determination would be made whether it would okay to put weight back on her ankles.

Days after her surgery, Derek told her about the results of the DNA test. She was just as shocked as Carlton when Derek told her that Liam was not Carlton's son. Breyonna never hinted once that Liam could be another man's child. It was bittersweet but one thing that Peyton, and Liam, could be assured of was that he had a father in Derek. That was one thing Peyton couldn't deny, Derek loved Liam like he was his own flesh and blood son. He would always be able to look back on his life and know that he was loved and cared for. She hoped and prayed that one day Liam would let go of his anger toward her for lying to him and forgive her.

What made things better for Peyton was Derek and Liam moved back into the house when she was discharged from the hospital. With Liam back at home, their relationship slowly became civil. Liam would come to her room and check in on her to see if she needed anything. He would even bring meals to her from time to time and sit and chat, even if it wasn't for long periods of time. Peyton felt hopeful. When she talked to him about his feelings concerning the DNA test results, he opened up more than he had in a long time.

"I'm glad Pastor Porter isn't my father," he admitted the day she convinced him to talk to her about the results. "I only have one dad and that's the way I wanted it. I prayed that prayer."

Peyton was surprised to hear her son say that he had prayed that Derek was his dad. He didn't act like he was too upset about never knowing who his biological father was.

"Will you forgive me for not telling you the truth about your birth mother and how I got you?" she asked him during the same conversation.

"I guess I forgive you. You are the only mother I've known, but you always talk about being honest and truthful, about how important it is for me to have integrity and good character, and all the time you were living a lie. You could have told me the truth, then none of this stuff with my birth mother would have happened. She wouldn't be dead and maybe we could have had a relationship. Now, because of you, I'll never have the chance to know her. Maybe she would have told me who my father is."

Peyton reached out to Liam from her wheelchair as he sat on the side of her bed. She laid her hand on top of his.

"I didn't want to lose my son. You're the only child I have. You mean the world to me, Liam. And I'm so sorry that I messed things up between us. My drinking played a role in my bad decisions too. I regret the way I handled everything."

"I'm not totally blaming you because I understand that you say I was in a bad situation when I was a little kid so I'm grateful that you wanted to get me out of that environment. I just don't understand why you didn't tell me. And then with you drinking all the time. I can't bring friends to the house because I don't know if you'll be drunk. It's embarrassing. You always say you're gonna stop, but you never do. You could have died in that accident, Ma. Those police officers could have died," Liam said sadly, not bothering to look at Peyton.

"You're right. I've messed up so many times. I planned on going to rehab, but one night, one more bad decision and look at where it landed me, in a wheelchair for God knows how long, Peyton cried, something she rarely did. "I'm sorry, Liam. I'm sorry for the drinking. I'm sorry that I lied to you and kept the truth from you and from Derek all these years. I guess I was afraid, afraid that you would want to leave and go be with Breyonna. I knew that wouldn't be good for you and I had lived a lie so long that I guess I didn't see the need to tell you or your father the truth. I couldn't have been more wrong."

The best thing that came out of that terrible day was Liam slowly began opening up. The signs were subtle, but Peyton clung to every moment that he came and stuck his head in her door to say hello. She took in every smile, every light hug he gave her as signs that their life as mother and son was on the mend.

As for Derek, the night of the accident, she thought there was a chance of them getting back together. But that night, like she always did, she managed to ruin any chance of that.

Not one to give up hope, she prayed that Derek's decision to move back in the house might lead to a reconciliation, but that was not the case. Derek made it clear that he was there to help her during her recuperation and give her and Liam a chance to strengthen their relationship. Outside of that, his intention was to file for divorce and ask for full custody of Liam.

25

"Misfortune tests the sincerity of friends." Aesop

Peyton sat in her bedroom, depressed about how she had made a mess of her marriage, her family, and her life. Her plans to enter rehab had been thwarted because of that one bad decision, and her marriage and chance for her family to be mended was no longer a possibility. Now she faced the possibility of being locked up. She had court coming up in a few days. Ryker said he would get the hearing put off until she was able to get up and around. Plus, he was working on getting the stiff charges reduced or dismissed altogether. Peyton knew the only way that would happen was if God stepped in and performed a miracle. Unlikely, after all she'd done.

Ryker arranged for at-home treatment for her alcohol addiction, and for the next ninety days a drug and alcohol counselor would visit her daily, set up a detox program and also connect with her through mandatory teleconferences.

The program was helping Peyton, but she still had that nagging urge for a drink. The very thing that had caused the major discord in her life was the very thing she still longed for. She was no better than a dope fiend.

If Derek went through with the divorce and took Liam, Peyton didn't know what her future would look like without the two most important men in her life, but once again, she made a promise to herself and God that she was going to make a change. Hopefully, it wouldn't be too late to make things right. Her parents had called when they learned the news about the accident and her injuries. Her mother was not pleased with Peyton, but then again, that was the story of Peyton's life. It was hard to do anything right in the eyes of her mother. After finding out that she would be fine over time, her mother scolded her each time she called until the point Peyton looked at her phone and disregarded the call when she saw it was her mother.

Peyton's father was somewhat more sympathetic. Unlike his wife, he was more concerned with Peyton's overall wellbeing and her marriage.

Peyton was glad they lived out of town and that she didn't see them often. Liam knew them but he rarely visited or spoke to his grandparents. They were still active seniors and did lots of overseas travel and went on cruises all the time, so they had little time for a kid under their feet.

Liam knocked lightly on his mother's bedroom door, temporarily giving Peyton a reprieve from the depressive state she was in.

"Yes?" Peyton responded to the knock and sat upright in the bed.

"Mom, Miss Avery is here."

The housewives had called the day before and arranged to pick her up for Ladies Day Out today. She agreed that she would go out with them, but she had changed her mind and didn't bother to tell them. Going out in a wheelchair wasn't exactly what she could see herself doing. The only times she had ventured outside of the house was when she had a doctor's appointment.

"Will you ask her to come up here, son?" Peyton said reluctantly.

"Yes, ma'am."

"What are you still doing in the bed? I told you I was going to pick you up and you said you would be ready."

"Yeah, I know, but I changed my mind. I'm sorry that I didn't call you. But I just can't do it. Will you tell the girls that I'll have to see them some other time, maybe when I get out of this chair," Peyton said pitifully.

"Peyton, staying up in this house can't be good for you. It's only going to keep you depressed. When was the last time you got out of the bed?"

"I get out the bed every day. I haven't gotten up today, other than to use the bathroom, because I just don't feel up to it, Avery."

"Because you're depressed. I've been there so I should know better than anyone." Avery sat down next to Peyton on the side of her bed. "Please, Peyton. You've got to try. You're shutting yourself off from me, Eva, and Meesha when you know we're your friends. We want to be here for you, but you won't let us."

"I know, and I'm sorry, but I just don't feel up to it. Give me another week or two. Okay?"

"So what do you want me to tell Eva and Meesha?"

"Just tell them I don't feel well, and that will be the truth. And I don't want to keep you girls from having fun. Trying to lug this wheelchair in and out of the trunk is not my idea of a good time."

"If the three of us can't get a wheelchair in and out of a trunk, I say something is wrong with us, so don't even try to use that as an excuse," Avery chastised her friend.

"I just want to be left alone."

"Well, I'm not going to do that. And since you won't go out, then I'm calling Eva and Meesha and we'll just have to have Ladies Day Out right up here in your bedroom."

"No, don't do that. Don't call them," Peyton cried out, reaching for Avery's hand to stop her from calling. "Please, Avery."

Avery ignored her plea and proceeded to call Eva. She told Eva what was going on and asked her to call Meesha. Avery still couldn't completely act her normal self when she was around Meesha. She avoided calling or texting her. She hadn't bothered Carlton and she believed that was in part due to the fact that she and Ryker were going to have a private marriage ceremony in the next few days. Her baby was growing in her belly and it showed. To know that she and Meesha were both pregnant with Carlton's babies was still a hard pill for her to swallow, but what made it even more difficult was the fact that she would have to keep the knowledge of that to herself. Of course, Avery didn't have proof that the baby inside of her was Carlton's but if her calculations were on point, then this *was* Carlton's kid.

Ryker didn't question her pregnancy because the last thing he would ever suspect or expect was for her to be unfaithful.

And he was right because before Carlton entered her life, she would never ever have stepped out on Ryker, married or not. She loved him just that much, but Carlton had a way about himself and one too many counseling sessions led to the two of them engaging in a sizzling affair. She thought she loved him, but lately, the more she thought of how Carlton so easily dismissed her and the child she was carrying, the more she realized that he had done nothing but use her like the men who used her back during her call girl days. He was no more than an unpaid John. And she had behaved like a deranged woman. Whenever she thought about it, she was ashamed of her stupid behavior.

The few times she'd seen Carlton since their meeting in the hotel parking lot, she could barely stand to look at him. He was the perfect definition of a wolf in sheep's clothing. Because of their breakup, she hadn't attended church in several Sundays, but that was about to play out, because Ryker believed in being a dedicated church goer. Something else she knew she had to do was work on treating Meesha better. Meesha had always been there for each one of them, and for her to suddenly become less than anything but nice to her, had begun to affect Avery. But it was hard because after all was said and done, part of her still thought that she would have a new and better life with Carlton. Avery shook her head as if she was trying to shake the thoughts right out of her mind.

Avery talked to both Eva and Meesha and the both of them agreed with Avery that they were going to help Peyton get out of the funk she was in.

"So Eva is going to prepare lunch," Avery told Peyton. "You know she loves to cook. And Meesha's going to bring a movie for us to watch," Avery laughed lightly. "So, there you have it. We're having Ladies Day Out at Eva's. And no need to rebel because going to Eva's is not the same as going out in public."

"Ohhh, okay," Peyton slowly agreed.

"Now, let's get you out of this bed and get you dressed."

Chapter 26

"Pain will leave you, when you let go." Jeremy Aldana

Eva spent the first half of her morning with Marissa, making up tasty Bolivian and American dishes for Ladies Day Out. The housewives had all agreed to come over to her house and she was excited to be able to entertain. It would help offset the boredom she experienced from being alone in the huge house. Except for the times she spent in the kitchen with Marissa, her days were filled pampering her dogs and reading.

Harper suggested that she enroll in culinary school because of her love for cooking, and the way her life was going, she thought that his suggestion might actually be a good idea. She had stopped volunteering at Perfecting Your Faith after Harper threw her out of the house. Her mind was far from desiring to help others when she was the one who needed help the most.

When he asked her to come back home, she expected things to return to normal, and return to normal proved to be an understatement. She heard somewhere before to be careful what you wish for. She didn't quite understand that American saying before, but now she understood fully well, because Harper's routine hadn't changed, except if being away from home now more than ever could constitute as change.

Eva finished the last dish, then went upstairs to shower and change before the housewives arrived.

An hour later she came back downstairs to relax a bit before the girls got there.

"Won't be home until late tonight. Don't wait up," the text from Harper read.

Eva threw her phone to the side. This made at least two weeks in a row that Harper didn't make it home until midnight. When he did come home, he took a shower and went to bed, sometimes even sleeping in one of the six other bedrooms rather than in the same bed with her. When she questioned him about his late nights and leaving her alone in their bed, he would tell her that he didn't want to disturb her. Eva was growing more frustrated day by day.

She picked up her phone and read the text again, making herself that much more upset.

She called him and to her surprise, he answered. "What is it, Eva? It's been a busy morning, so I don't have much time to talk."

"I don't understand why you have to be home late every night, Harper."

"I don't have time for this, Eva. I'm a busy man. You know what I do. That hasn't changed. So, will you get over your tantrum and do something useful with your life. Have you checked into culinary school like I suggested? Maybe then you wouldn't be clinging on to me like a blood sucking leech," he said, sounding irritated.

"I thought things would be different when you asked me to come back home, but you're away even more."

"You want to keep living the lifestyle you lead, then let me do my job. You know that I'm writing another book and I may be signing up to have another television show. So what I'm telling you is you're going to see me even less than you do now. Now if you can't handle that, then you might want to think about whether you'd rather go back to Bolivia with your family or you can do something useful with your life. I'm getting a little sick and tired of taking care of them anyway. Maybe if you finish school you can foot the bill for them instead of me."

Eva grew insanely angry. "Are you threatening to cut my family's money off? You promised me when you married me that you would always make sure they were well provided for."

"And I've kept my word. It's you who chose to open your legs up for another man, so you should be glad I was willing to take you back and to keep supporting your family. I'll even pay for you to go to school. I already give you the best of everything and you still aren't satisfied. I'm trying to do what God wants me to do and that's to keep this marriage together.

But don't expect me to walk around like I have a sweet, innocent wife when if truth be told, you're a whore. Be glad I want you, Eva. Now, like I said, I'm busy." She heard a dead silence and looked at her phone. Harper had hung up.

The doorbell rang. *"Obtendré la puerta (I'll get the door),"* Marissa said out loud to Eva as she came up the long hall.

She opened the door. *"Buenas dias, come in, por favor,"* Marissa said to Avery, Meesha, and Peyton.

"Good afternoon, Marissa," the ladies said one by one.

Meesha pushed Peyton inside the house. Marissa stepped up to assist.

"Thank you, Marissa, but I can manage," Meesha politely said.

"Hi, there," Eva said, appearing in the foyer. Marissa went outside to make sure everything was set for the luncheon

"I thought we'd eat outside since it's such a beautiful day."

"That's fine," Avery said and the ladies followed Eva to the beautifully landscaped backyard and outdoor kitchen and living space.

The ladies sat down while Peyton maneuvered her wheelchair so that her back was against the sun.

Marissa and Eva served non-alcoholic fruit drinks so as not to tempt Peyton. Peyton had done remarkably well with her in-home alcohol treatment program. She'd lost at least ten pounds, and taken a bold step and had her hair dyed black. She looked like a different Peyton.

The women exchanged their usual banter until the conversations turned serious as each woman shared what was going on in their lives.

"When are you going to be able to put weight on your legs?" Eva asked Peyton.

"Last week made eight weeks that I've been trapped in this chair. I went to my doctor the day before yesterday and he told me I would have to stay off my legs another four weeks. I'm so pissed," she spouted.

"I'm so sorry," said Eva.

"Yeah, that's terrible," Avery said. "I know you were looking forward to being able to get up at least some of the time."

"It could be worse," Meesha reminded Peyton and the others. "You could not be able to walk at all. You had some serious fractures, Peyton. And four weeks will pass in a flash."

"I guess you do have a point," said Avery. "I can't believe it's been eight weeks already."

"Well, none of you are stuck in a chair either so it's easy for y'all to say," she remarked.

"I still agree with Meesha, four weeks will come and go before you know it, and hopefully you'll be up walking around, even if it's a little."

"I wish I felt the same about this load I'm carrying," Avery laughed, placing a hand around her basketball sized belly.

Meesha laughed too, rubbing her own belly. "Tell me about it. It's not easy being pregnant in the summer. The Florida heat can wear a pregnant woman out."

Eva stood up, and walked over to the outside kitchen area. Like clockwork, Marissa reappeared and helped her prepare the food to serve.

After getting their food, they oohed and aahed over how good it was while they continued talking.

"How are things going with you and Harper?"

Eva stopped eating momentarily and reluctantly began to share the latest news about her and Harper.

"You mean to tell me this dude threatened to stop helping your parents?"

"And he wants to pounce up in here late at night whenever he wants. I don't care what he says, it's not that much going on at Adverse General that will keep him away from home until midnight every night," Peyton complained.

"I don't understand why he doesn't sleep with you in the same bed," Avery told her.

Eva looked around to make sure Marissa had left. She had. Tears formed in her eyes. "I'm beginning to regret moving back. Maybe I should have moved into one of those houses we were looking at, Peyton."

"I don't know what to say. And you say he's called you out of your name, too," Meesha remarked.

"Yes," Eva said, crying and wiping her tears at the same time.

"I think you should take his advice," Peyton suddenly said.

"What advice?" Avery asked and looked at Eva.

"Are you talking about me enrolling in culinary school?" Eva said, wiping the last few tears from her eyes and recomposing herself.

"Yes," replied Peyton.

"Yeah, that does sound like a good idea. It will get you out of the house and you'll be doing something you love," Meesha added.

"After you're done you can make him foot the bill for you to open your own restaurant, then dump his tail." Peyton laughed.

"If he's going to get back into television and writing another book, that only means he's going to be away from home that much more, if that's even possible," said Avery. "I feel so bad for you, Eva."

"I say look into going to culinary school. Get a life of your own," Peyton retorted.

"Maybe you all are right." Eva cleared her eyes and sounded like she had regained some strength in just that short period of time after listening to her friends.

"Let me know if I can help you in any way. We can start looking for the best culinary schools in Miami and Adverse City," Avery offered.

"Thanks. I appreciate that."

"How are you and Ryker?" Eva turned the questions to Avery.

"I've never been happier. He seems like a different person. I finally believe that we're going to be just fine," she said, inwardly glowing and basking in the fact that in a few days she would officially become Mrs. Ryker Mitchelson. She didn't divulge her secret to the housewives since they always believed that she and Ryker were already married. "I feel like God has given me a second chance. For a while, I had gotten somewhat off course. I was doing things I never thought I would do."

"Care to go into detail?" Meesha asked.

Avery shook her head from side to side. "No, I don't think so, but let's just say that God opened my eyes before it was too late. I thank him every day for it, too."

"Good for you," Meesha said, reaching over next to her and squeezing Avery's hand.

"Okay, what's happening with you, Meesha?" Peyton spoke up next.

"I guess I'm like Avery. Things are pretty much back to normal in the Porter household. As you know, Liam is not Carlton's son. And, I don't mean this in a bad way, but Peyton, I'm so glad that the DNA results were done and that it proved Liam is not Carlton's kid."

"No need to apologize to me. I'm sorry that you had to go through the whole mess from the beginning. I just hate the way I did things and I also hate that my son will never know who his biological father is."

"Yes, but he has Derek, and we always say it, Derek is a good father," Eva said.

"Yeah," Peyton said.

"Now that all of that's over with, I can't wait until this little girl pops out, and as far as Carlton and me, I think we're in a good place again. I can't say that I fully trust him, but I'm getting there."

"Whoa, whoa, whoa," Peyton said, raising her hand and showing her palm. "Did you say little girl? How do you know it's a girl? Speculating?"

"Nope. This one is a girl." Meesha laughed. "Me, Carlton, and the boys went together to find out a couple of weeks ago. I was waiting until we were all together to tell you. So, it's a girl!"

"Yayyyy," said Eva.

"Congratulations," Avery said in a more cordial tone than she had recently.

"That child is going to be rotten to the high heavens," Peyton added and laughed. "She's going to have Carlton and the boys wrapped around her little finger."

"Yeah, I think so," said Meesha happily. " So, how are you doing, Peyton, besides dealing with those fractured ankles?"

"To be honest, I haven't felt this good in a long time. At first I was against the Skype sessions with a psychologist, but now I look forward to them. The psychologist has helped me understand a lot about myself and why I drank, so that part is going great. She's helping me learn how to better communicate with Liam, too. Our relationship is on the mend. She's even had him sit in on some of the Skype sessions, along with Derek."

"So are you and Derek working through things too?" Eva asked with curiosity.

Peyton paused then shook her head. "No, not really. We talked but I think he's still leaning toward a divorce. He says our marriage is too damaged. But he hasn't moved out, and as far as I know, he doesn't plan to."

"He wants a divorce but he wants to remain in the house with his ex-wife. How do you feel about that?" Meesha asked.

"Yeah, how do you feel?" asked Avery.

"If we can reside in the same house without bickering then it's cool with me. God knows the house is big enough for us to have our own separate spaces and not infringe on one another. I think it would be healthy for Liam to have both of us there. I don't want him to have to face anymore separation of any kind. You know what I mean?"

"I think I do," said Avery. "He's a teenage boy, and I don't care what some people say, a boy needs his father in his life."

"Yea, I agree," said Meesha.

"Me too," said Eva.

"What about the court case? What's the latest on that?" Meesha asked.

"Well Ryker is still working on getting me probation. He's confident that he will. And what I'm about to share with you all cannot go out of this room," Peyton emphasized, "I'll have to pay a pretty hefty fine. You know he's the one who arranged my in-house alcohol treatment. But the thing is we've already made an undisclosed out of court settlement to both officers. Girls, I tell you, that Ryker is something else," added Peyton.

"Yep, he is." Avery beamed with pride.

"*Aaand* he set up college funds for both officers' minor children, reimbursed them for time off of their jobs, and paid them substantial lump sums for their personal injuries. How he was able to settle this part already is beyond me." Peyton did a Wendy Williams throw of the hands. "I don't question him. Whatever he does to keep me from going to jail and satisfy the courts I'm grateful. That's all I can say." Peyton smiled and shook her head then picked up her fruity drink and took a sip.

"If anyone can do it, Ryker can," Avery said.

"Thank God for money," Eva added.

"You said it," Peyton agreed. "It may not be able to buy some things, but it sure can buy a lot."

The girls all laughed.

"It still amazes me what having money and knowing the right people, with the right connections can do," Meesha commented.

"Yep, and Ryker deserves every penny he gets. He's definitely earned every right to be the highly sought after attorney that he is in Adverse City and in Miami Beach, Florida," said Peyton as the other ladies nodded in agreement.

Silence penetrated their banter and the ladies enjoyed the remainder of their food and drinks.

The ladies ended Ladies Day Out with reminding Eva that she should start putting her own life in her hands and enroll in school.

As they got ready to leave, Meesha said, "I hope I see all of you at church this coming Sunday. I don't remember the last time we were all there at the same time. No matter what we've been through, we owe God some of our time because through everything, he's never left our sides."

"I can't deny that," Avery said.

"I plan to be there. That's one place Harper insists on going you know. The church house but he won't come to this house." Eva laughed lightly.

Peyton rolled herself to the front door and then stopped to wait on help from her friends the remainder of the way. She said, "I can't promise you that I'll be there, but I'm sure going to make an effort, because when I think of how differently things could have panned out for me, I know it was nothing but God who brought me through."

"Well, looks like Sunday is our next date," Meesha said and the housewives began to embrace one another as they left.

Chapter 27

"Life has many ways of testing a person's will, either by having nothing happen at all or by having everything happen all at once." Paulo Coelho

Today was Avery's official wedding day. Ryker went all out by chartering a private plane to fly them to Las Vegas. Avery hadn't experienced this side of Ryker since before their first daughter, Lexie, was born.

A limousine was waiting at the private airport when the plane landed and they were whisked off to the luxurious Four Seasons Hotel on the iconic Las Vegas strip.

Avery didn't have much time to settle into the room before Ryker told her it was time for his second surprise, a "Time for Two" Couples Spa treatment that included a three hour couple's massage, couple's facial, chocolate covered strawberries and champagne for two. It was the best experience ever for Avery.

The weekend continued to get better and better because after a night of passionate and intense lovemaking, despite her big belly, she woke up to the most beautiful sunrise and 360 degree panoramic views of the Las Vegas Strip, a huge perk of the twenty two hundred square feet Presidential Strip-View Suite. After a shower together, they enjoyed breakfast in their room.

"Ryker, I'm absolutely floored," she said, kissing him as they walked downstairs to the front of the hotel to a limousine waiting to take them to the courthouse to get their marriage license and then to The Primrose Courtyard at the Wynn Hotel for an intimate, just for two, wedding ceremony.

At the Wynn, Ryker had arranged a minister to officiate the ceremony. He had spared no expense and covered every detail with the help of a wedding consultant at the hotel. Red roses lined the courtyard.

"You deserve it, Avery. You're the mother of my children."

"Is that the only reason you made me your wife? Because of our children."

"Of course not. I love you Avery. I know I haven't always shown it, but I do. I should have done this a long time ago."

I don't want to think about shoulda, woulda, coulda. I only want to bask in the memories we're making now. This weekend couldn't be more perfect."

Ω

Meesha walked along the beach and watched the majestic waves as they kissed the shore. The coolness of the sand between her toes mixed with the foamy water was tranquil.

Strolling along the beach, all alone, she felt one with God. Moments like this helped to calm her spirit. So much had happened over the past year that had troubled her. It hadn't exactly made her question her faith in God, but she did feel as if she had somehow let God down. She hadn't sought him as much as she once did because she allowed the circumstances she was going through in her marriage to take precedence over her relationship with God.

She stopped momentarily, her maxi dress swaying against the wind, and her weaved hair blowing like the sails on the sailboats she viewed out on the ocean.

"God, I'm sorry," she said as she studied the waves and realized their power. She caressed her swelling belly as she continued to gaze out in the ocean. Far as her eyes could see there was water. She likened that to faith. Looking out, though she could not see a speck of land, of life, only the vast ocean, she knew that somewhere beyond her visible sight there was life. Faith was believing in that which the eye cannot see.

Father God, give me the strength I need, the faith I once had to know that you are in full control," she prayed. "Bless my family, this baby inside of me, my sons, and my husband.

Help me to make the right decisions and help him to do the same.

Heal my friend, Peyton, and give direction to Avery and Eva." Meesha smiled as she felt the slightest movement of her belly. She took it as a sign from God that he was yet by her side. The child inside tapped lightly against her tummy again. Just that tiny movement gave Meesha a reassurance that everything would be all right.

Chapter 28

"The marks humans leave are too often scars." John Green

"Welcome this morning, people of God," Carlton said in a booming voice. "If you know that God is good, let me hear you say Praise the Lord."

The sanctuary full of people repeated, "Praise the Lord."

"It's good to be in the house of the Lord. I want you to open your Bibles or pull up on your phones and tablets to Romans twelve verse two. The King James Version reads, And be not conformed to this world: but be ye transformed by the renewing of your mind, that ye may prove what is that good, and acceptable, and perfect, will of God. That word transformed means 'changed'. There are many verses and accounts about change in the Bible. I've heard it said on many occasions that the only way to deal with change is when you are the one doing the changing. Change is inevitable. The more you live the more things are subject to change," Carlton preached. "But it can be hard to change. Many times, we become comfortable with the way things are, and we kick and fight against change like a kid having a temper tantrum."

Carlton looked out in the filled sanctuary at the face of his First Lady and his four sons lined on their reserved second row pew. He looked directly behind them and there sat Avery, Ryker and their two daughters. Next to them sat Liam and Derek with Peyton's chair parked in the aisle. And next there was Eva and Harper.

"I thank the good Lord for change. Change can help you grow. Change can help you become all that God has designed for you to become. Change can help you step into your life's destiny. You may say, Pastor Porter I don't want things to change. Everything is fine just the way it is. I understand you because you see oftentimes change disrupts, stirs up, and coughs up things and situations that we don't care to face or want to face."

Carlton continued, becoming more fired up as he spoke. "Did you know that in order to receive salvation, you have to make a change? You have to repent. Repent means to change your mind. To stop doing what you were doing or living the way you were living and ask God to come into your heart and change you.

I must confess," Carlton said, looking in Avery's direction then at Meesha, "I had to do some serious changing myself. I was headed down a path of destruction and I was taking people down that destructive path with me. I thank God that He changed my way of thinking before it was too late."

Avery nodded in agreement.

Carlton preached for the next twenty minutes. He saw Avery's swelling belly and thoughts of the child she carried inside filled his mind in the midst of his sermon. That baby could very well be his yet he'd made Avery swear that she would not reveal what they'd done in the dark.

He closed his sermon by saying, "I'm asking you to forgive me. Forgive me for my sins, oh, Lord." He looked out at Avery once again. "Forgive me for hidden secrets and wrong doings." He thought of Breyonna and the mess she'd made of her life….and his. He thought of the harm that had come to her in the form of drugs and even her tragic death.

"Forgive me, Lord for the harm I brought against others, some intentional and others unintentional," he confessed before his flock. "Change me, Father God. Restore a renewed spirit within me. Give me a clean heart," he spoke as he became increasingly emotional.

Clinging to every word Carlton spoke, Avery rubbed her belly in a circular motion as Ryker placed his arm around her.

Meesha allowed pinned up tears to cascade down her cheeks.

Peyton cried softly and Liam's hand gently patted his mother's hand.

Eva felt Harper's hand swallow hers inside of his and she gently pulled back, thinking about the next phase of her life and the change she was now ready to make.

So much more lies ahead for The Real Housewives of Adverse City. So much more is left of their stories. Only time will tell where their lives lead them next.

Coming 2018 The Real Housewives of Adverse City 3

Words from the Author

What can I say other than once again it is evident that money, even when you have lots of it, cannot buy happiness, peace of mind, and love. At least not real happiness, peace of mind, and love. Shucks, as you've read here money can't even buy faithfulness and commitment.

The fact remains, we are all flawed. We all have issues. We all have something we are dealing with and it makes no difference what our bank account states. Life is so unpredictable. Things can change on the drop of a dime (no pun intended.) Life happens whether we have fat bank accounts or whether our bank accounts are in the negative. Blessings rain down on the just as well as the unjust.

The women (and the men) in this series experience it all. They are put to the test and their money and prestige cannot bring them what they long for. Those intangible things like the love of family and friends. It can't bring trust and integrity. It can't induce good character.

I tend to believe that whatever type of person you are, and I mean really and truly are, then having money only magnifies it. If you're mean and evil when you have nothing, then guess what? You're more times than not going to be mean and evil with a lot of money. If you're sneaky and of low character and morals, then guess what? You're going to be even sneakier with low character and morals. On the other hand, if you're kind, generous, and loving, then more than likely you will be the same if you have millions of dollars like the characters in this series.

To thy own self be true. Be true to who you are. Learn to treat others with love, kindness, and respect. Always go about trying your best to do what is right, what is pure, what is lovely, what is of good report.

Adversity comes in all of our lives. How will you handle it?

Thanks again, Readers for supporting me by purchasing and reading my books. There is no me without YOU and there is no US without HIM!

Love ya,

Shelia
God's Amazing Girl

More Titles by Shelia Bell
Some titles are written under former name of Shelia Lipsey

YA/Teen Titles
House of Cars
The Life of Payne
The Lollipop Girl

Standalone Novels
Show A Little Love (*out of print*)
Always Now and Forever Love Hurts
Into Each Life
Sinsatiable
What's Blood Got To Do With It?
Only In My Dreams

Series Books

Beautiful Ugly
True Beauty (*sequel to Beautiful Ugly*)

My Son's Wife Series
My Son's Wife
My Son's Ex-Wife: The Aftermath
My Son's Next Wife
My Sister My Momma My Wife
My Wife My Baby...And Him
The McCoys of Holy Rock
Dem McCoy Boys

Adverse City Series
The Real Housewives of Adverse City
The Real Housewives of Adverse City 2
The Real Housewives of Adverse City 3

Anthologies
Bended Knees
Weary to Will

Learning to Love Me

Contact information
www.sheliaebell.net
www.sheliawritesbooks.com
sheliawritesbooks@yahoo.com
www.facebook.com/sheliawritesbooks
@sheliaebell (Twitter)
www.instagram.com/sheliaebell
www.instagram.com/literacyrocks (Instagram)
@bwabclitfest (twitter